Amy Anne Hilliard Was Not The Most Beautiful Woman Doug Had Ever Seen.

But there was an aura about her that made him catch his breath each time he laid eyes on her.

It made him catch his breath this time, too. Yet something was different. Very different.

The obvious signs of stress and strain made him ache. They also made him angry. If Amy had been within touching distance, he would have been torn between desire to sweep her into his arms and hold her safe, and the impulse to grab her by the shoulders and shake some sense into her.

Amy... Amy... Doug thought. *What's happened to you?*

He started toward her.

A heartbeat later, Amy turned her head and spotted him.

Douglas Maxwell Browne was not the most handsome man Amy had ever seen. But there was an aura about him that made her catch her breath each time she laid eyes on him.

It made her catch her breath this time, too. Yet something was different. Very different...

Dear Reader:

Welcome to Silhouette Desire—sensual, compelling, believable love stories written by and for today's woman. When you open the pages of a Silhouette Desire, you open yourself up to a new world—a world of promising passion and endless love.

Each and every Silhouette Desire is a wonderful love story that is both sensual *and* emotional. You're with the hero and heroine each and every step of the way—from their first meeting, to their first kiss...to their happy ending. You'll experience all the deep joys—and occasional tribulations—of falling in love.

In future months, look for terrific Silhouette Desire romances from some of your favorite authors, such as Annette Broadrick, Dixie Browning, Nancy Martin and Lass Small, just to name a few.

So go wild with Desire. You'll be glad you did!

Lucia Macro
Senior Editor

CAROLE BUCK

TIME ENOUGH FOR LOVE

SILHOUETTE *Desire*

Published by Silhouette Books New York

America's Publisher of Contemporary Romance

SILHOUETTE BOOKS
300 East 42nd St., New York, N.Y. 10017

ISBN: 0-373-05565-X

First Silhouette Books printing May 1990

Printed in the U.S.A.

CAROLE BUCK

is a television news writer and movie reviewer who lives in Atlanta. She is single. Her hobbies include cake decorating, ballet and traveling. She collects frogs, but does not kiss them. Carole says she's in love with life; she hopes the books she writes reflect this.

Prologue

Doug Browne had always prided himself on finding time for things that mattered. Staying in shape was one of those things. That's why he made a point of shoehorning a daily workout into his busy schedule.

"C'mon, buddy," his current accomplice in athleticism urged in a weary but good-humored voice. "Finish me off."

Doug glanced sideward at Paul Lansing. The enemy. One of his closest friends in the world, too... *off* the squash court.

He sucked in a deep breath, discovering that he had an oddly difficult time forcing the much-needed air into his laboring lungs. A drop of perspiration trickled down his face. He swiped at his forehead with the back of his hand. His arm seemed strangely heavy. He was vaguely conscious of a kind of cramping in his fingers, too.

Doug shook his head. For an instant, everything wavered and blurred. It was as though his brain had temporarily disconnected.

"Doug?" Paul Lansing asked.

Doug grimaced and shook his head again. Cripes, he thought disgustedly. What's going on with me today? Is Laser Brain Browne losing it on the squash court?

Laser Brain? The phrase stopped him cold for a moment. Now, where—?

Laser Brain. Of course! Lord, it had been years since he'd thought of that nickname, much less heard anyone use it.

Amy had first called him that—what? Two decades ago? No. A little longer than that now. She'd gotten the idea from something their junior-high-school science teacher had said in class one day.

Laser Brain. The appellation dated from the period in their relationship when adolescent embarrassment over their mutual attraction had demanded that they verbally abuse each other at every possible opportunity. Secretly Doug had been flattered by the designation. Not that he'd ever come close to admitting such a thing to Amy. Good Lord, no! Instead, he'd retaliated by calling her—

"Doug?"

Startled, Doug put a leash on his wayward thoughts and hauled them back into the present. He looked across the court.

"Are you okay, Doug?" Paul asked.

"Yeah—" The word seemed to stick in Doug's throat. He swallowed and tried again. "I'm fine, Paul." The words echoed against the walls of the court. They sounded odd to him. As though they'd been coated with fuzz.

"Well, you don't look—"

"I'm fine!" Doug insisted sharply. He squeezed the small, hard ball he was holding once...twice...three times, then bounced up and down on the toes of his feet. "I'm fine," he repeated, and pivoted away.

This is game point, he reminded himself, centering his weight and narrowing his concentration. I'm going to win this if it kills me.

It was only a figure of speech. A phrase he'd invoked countless times before, when fueling his determination to finish first—to come out on top. He didn't mean it. Not really.

Not *really*...

Afterward, Doug wondered if he'd finally tempted fate once too often. He wondered if someone—or something—had heard his silent pledge and decided to take him up on it.

Game point. Ready, set—

Suddenly, two invisible arms wrapped themselves around Doug's chest and began to squeeze. It was as though a sumo wrestler was trying to give him a hug.

A crushing pressure settled on his breastbone.

Doug's knees started to buckle. He dropped the racket he was holding and heard it clatter against the smoothly polished floor of the court. Sweat poured off his face. His stomach roiled violently. The acrid taste of bile polluted his mouth.

"Doug—" Paul Lansing was beside him now, his exertion-flushed face taut with concern. Doug felt his friend's hands clasp him, trying to offer support. "What is it?"

Bambi...Meets...Godzilla, he thought grimly.

What?

Bambi Meets—

Oh...God. Oh, yes. Years ago at college he and Amy had gone to a cartoon film festival. One of the animated shorts had been titled *Bambi Meets Godzilla*. It had opened with a delicately drawn deer frolicking about on the screen to some sweet classical tune. Then abruptly a monstrous foot had descended from the top of the screen and squished the dainty fawn. After a second or so, the creature's toenails had retracted and the credits had started to roll.

At this moment, Douglas Maxwell Browne had a pretty good idea of how little Bambi must have felt lying smashed beneath Godzilla's humongous foot. He was heartily sorry he'd laughed at the cartoon.

Had Amy laughed? No. No, she hadn't. She'd turned her face into his shoulder going, "Ooooo, how sick!" instead. Doug could remember how her fragrant, silky hair had teased the underside of his chin and how the soft weight of her breasts had brushed against—

"Doug." It was Paul again. And somebody was with him. No, make that two...uh, *three* somebodies. "Take it easy, okay? Just stay calm. We're going to get you to a hospital. I think you're having a heart attack."

A heart attack?

Doug rejected the idea instantly.

A heart attack?

No way. Impossible. Couldn't happen.

Doug Browne didn't have a heart. He'd given it away years ago to the woman he'd loved and lost.

He'd given it to Amy.

His ex-wife...Amy.

"Doug!"

Amy Hilliard awoke suddenly, invoking her ex-husband's name with a panicky gasp.

Oh...God. Oh. Something—someone—was sitting on her chest. Pressing. Bearing down.

Her heart was pounding. She could scarcely breathe.

It was dark. Pitch black. Everything was closing in on her. She felt trapped. She had to...she had to...

Amy struggled to a sitting position, kicking at the sheets that entangled her. She fumbled for the lamp on the nightstand next to the bed. Her fingers encountered a stack of papers, knocking it over. This set off a chain reaction. She heard something fall off the nightstand and land on the thickly carpeted floor with a dull thud.

Please. Oh, please.

Her hands were trembling.

Light. She had to have some light!

Amy heard someone whimpering and realized it must be her.

She gave a sob of relief as she finally found the lamp switch and clicked it on. The sudden flare of illumination was almost blindingly bright as she blinked repeatedly as her eyes tried to adjust. Her lashes were wet, as though she'd been crying.

Amy brought her unsteady hands up to her chest, feeling the still frantic hammering of her heart. She inhaled shakily. Her temples throbbed sickeningly. Her mouth was cottony and filled with the unpleasant taste of fear.

She exhaled, rocking forward and back, willing herself to relax.

Breathe in . . . breathe out.

Relax.

Breathe in . . . breathe out.

Amy massaged her jaw. She could tell she'd been grinding her teeth in her sleep again. Her dentist had warned her about that. He'd told her she didn't have any layers of enamel left to spare.

Amy turned her head from side to side, her blunt-cut, coppery-brown hair shifting against her neck with each movement. She could feel a few strands clinging to her perspiration-sheened temples and cheeks. One corner of her mind noted that her nightgown was damp, too.

Teeth-grinding and night sweats. Oh, that was just wonderful!

Amy supposed she should have expected something like this. She'd been running in the red zone for over a year now—pushing herself harder and further and faster than she'd ever thought possible. She'd reached the point where doing only three things at the same time seemed like sheer, unadulterated laziness. It had been months since she'd had eight straight hours of sleep and even longer than that since she'd taken a full weekend off.

And now here she was in Tokyo on the verge of locking up the biggest deal of her career. She'd been jet-lagged as well as just plain exhausted when she'd arrived from Los Angeles. But instead of being able to go straight to bed, she'd had to be bright-eyed and bushy-tailed during a long evening of being saki'd and sushi'd by several of her Japanese counterparts.

No wonder she'd woken up in a panic at—Amy glanced toward the clock on the bedside stand—two-fifteen in the morning! No wonder she'd been grinding her teeth, sweating and having a bad dream.

Correction. Not a "bad dream." A *nightmare*. She'd been having a genuine nightmare. And not the usual anxiety-driven one about walking into a vitally important negotiating session totally naked and completely unprepared, either. No. This one had been about Doug.

Doug, who was half a world away in New York City and—she glanced at the clock again and made some time-conversion calculations—probably sweating through his daily workout at this very moment.

Amy's heart lurched suddenly and a disturbing shiver danced through her nervous system. She worried her lower lip with her teeth for a second or two, wrestling with a strange sense of apprehension. Why did she have the feeling that something awful had happened?

Surrendering to impulse, Amy reached for the phone. She punched in a long sequence of digits, then jammed the receiver between her left shoulder and ear. Twiddling with a lock of hair, she waited impatiently through the click-whir-clicks of various international connections.

"Allen, Chandler, Marchand and Lee," a feminine voice with a crisp British inflection finally announced. "Mr. Browne's office."

"Margaret?" Amy asked. "This is Amy Hilliard. Is he in, please?"

"Oh, Ms. Hilliard." The cool voice on the other end warmed a little. "No, I am sorry. He's out of the office at the moment."

Amy took some comfort from this very routine answer. If anything had happened to Doug, Margaret would have known about it. "He—is he at the athletic club, then?" she queried.

"Well, he *did* mention something about a squash game with Dr. Lansing." A small, well-bred laugh accompanied this admission. "Is there anything I can do for you?"

"Ah, no," Amy responded after a moment. Although she was feeling better physically, she was still conscious of a gnawing sense of uneasiness. "But thank you for asking, Margaret. I was...that is..." She shook her head. "Oh, never mind. It's nothing important. If you'd just tell Doug that I—ah—"

Tell Doug what? Amy demanded of herself. Tell him I'm in Tokyo having nightmares? Tell him I miss him? Tell him...tell him I still love him?

Any one of those messages would have been accurate and Amy knew it. But none was appropriate for a woman to give her ex-husband's very proper English secretary and Amy knew that, too.

"Ms. Hilliard?" Margaret prompted helpfully.

Amy cradled her forehead in her palm. "Please, just tell him I called."

One

Roses.

Long-stemmed . . . blush-pink . . . roses.

One dozen of them, in full and fragrant bloom.

That was about the last thing in the world Amy Hilliard expected to find waiting in her Manhattan hotel room when she checked in after a flight from Los Angeles.

The exquisite sight and scent of them left her dazed and dizzy.

There was no card, but that didn't matter. Only one man had ever sent her blush-pink roses. Only one man.

But it had been a long time since he'd last done so. Much—too much, probably—had changed since then.

I'm hallucinating, Amy decided quite calmly. Somehow that notion seemed more acceptable than the idea that her ex-husband had surprised her with a gift of her favorite flowers. Some people hear voices. I see—and smell—blush-pink roses. But if I just shut my eyes and take a few deep breaths—

"Nice roses," the bellman observed pleasantly as he carefully deposited her leather suitcase on the rack provided.

Amy's eyes flew open. "Y-yes," she agreed faintly. "Yes . . . they are."

All right. So, she wasn't hallucinating. The roses were real. They were real, and they were as bewildering as they were beautiful. Because, to put it plainly, Amy Anne Hilliard didn't have the foggiest idea why Douglas Maxwell Browne would want to give her much of *anything* anymore—much less a dozen blush-pink roses.

It was such an emotionally evocative gesture. So extravagant.

So totally unlike him.

No, not *totally* unlike him, Amy conceded, an odd tremor skittering along the nerve endings just beneath her skin. After all, she could remember back to a time when Doug had courted her with posies and poetry, to a time when he'd stood beneath her dormitory window during a snowstorm and serenaded—

"Ma'am?" The bellman's inquiry severed the web of memories she was spinning. His tone was deferential, but tinged with a hint of concern.

Amy shook her head, forcing herself to resist the seductive lure of the past. Times had changed. So had she. So had Doug.

"Sorry," she murmured, squaring her slim shoulders and snapping open her trim, envelope-style bag.

"Is there something I can do?"

She shook her head again, extracting several dollars from her wallet. The bills were crisp and new and crackled against her fingers. "No," she said calmly, extending the money. "Thank you."

The bellman seemed to hesitate a moment, his features contracting into a frown. Then suddenly his face smoothed into a neutral expression. He accepted her tip and pocketed it with a practiced gesture. "Thank *you*, ma'am," he responded. "Now, if you need anything, just call the front desk."

Amy nodded. She saw the man's eyes move from her to the roses and back again.

"Must be a special day for you, hmm?" he asked quietly.

Amy could no more have kept from glancing at the flowers than iron filings could defy a magnet.

"Must be," she murmured.

Roses.

Long-stemmed . . . blush-pink . . . roses.

One dozen of them, in full and fragrant bloom.

Doug Browne shifted restlessly, drumming his fingertips against the top of his desk and picturing the flowers he had so carefully selected that afternoon.

He wasn't second-guessing himself about what he'd done. He had finished second-guessing hours ago. He was at the fourth- or fifth-guessing stage, at this point.

I should have included a card, he thought irritably. Nothing too pushy. Nothing too personal. Maybe one of my business cards with a message.

He snapped off this line of thought with a growl of frustration. He stood up, shoved back his chair and began to pace around his office.

Not a *business* card, for God's sake! he berated himself, jerking at the knot in his tie as though he were loosening a hangman's noose. Amy's not a client! This is not an exercise in networking. I should have included one of those cards from the florist's shop. Yeah. I should have signed my name to one of those cards and sent it along, just to make sure.

Doug came to a full stop.

Just to make sure of what? he demanded. Just to make sure that Amy knows who the roses are from?

His hands clenched into fists. He was conscious of a sudden throbbing in his right temple.

She'd damned well better know who they're from, he decided angrily. Even without a card! Who else would send her blush-pink roses? Who the hell else? I'm the only one. The only one. Haven't I *always* sent her—

Doug exhaled abruptly, feeling like a man who'd just collided with a brick wall and had the wind knocked out of him. Running up against the truth—something he'd found himself doing with increasing frequency during the past month-and-a-half—tended to have that effect on him.

The truth was, he *hadn't* always sent Amy blush-pink roses. And that, in a peculiar way, summed up why the two of them were now divorced and living on opposite sides of the country.

Doug raked his fingers through his dark hair. He drew in a deep breath, then slowly expelled it. Oh, Amy, he thought. Why didn't I understand what was happening to us when it was happening? We started out so close, but we ended up so far apart. And neither of us realized until it was too late.

No, dammit! Doug swore silently. It couldn't be too late. *It couldn't be!*

Abruptly he pivoted on his heel and crossed back to his document-littered desk. He picked up the phone. He hit nine to get an outside line, then rapidly punched in seven more digits. There was no hesitation. He'd memorized this particular phone number hours before.

One ring. Two rings. Pick up. A polite spiel of greeting followed by a pause.

"Good evening. This is Mr. Browne again," Doug said into the expectant silence. "Could you please tell me whether Ms. Hilliard—Ms. Amy Hilliard—has checked in yet?"

The roses were making Amy crazy.

Once she'd gotten over the initial shock of pleasure and puzzlement they'd given her, she'd decided to try to put the flowers out of her mind and go about her business. After the bellman had left, she'd kicked off her pumps, peeled down to her underwear, then plunked herself and the contents of her briefcase on her hotel bed. She had work to do and she was going to do it!

Sure she was. And when she finished it, she was going to study singing for a few hours so she could star at the Metropolitan Opera.

Amy pulled off her horn-rimmed reading glasses and tossed them, plus the prospectus she'd been pretending to review, aside. Crossing her bare arms over her lingerie-clad breasts, she heaved a frustrated sigh. Then, reluctantly, she turned her head to look at Doug's roses.

Why had he sent them? she wondered for the umpteenth time. *Why?*

Amy used her big toe to nudge the leather-bound appointment book lying by her right foot. She knew the answer wasn't in there. She'd looked. Several times.

All right. Run through the possibilities once again.

It certainly wasn't her birthday. She'd turned thirty-five—or as she preferred to characterize it, celebrated her twenty-ninth birthday for the seventh time—three months before.

Some kind of anniversary? Today *was* May 16.

She and Doug had exchanged wedding vows in the second week of July nearly thirteen years before. Scratch that from the list.

They'd signed the divorce papers ending more than a decade of marriage during the third week of October. Take that occasion out of the running, too.

May 16 . . . May 16 . . .

Their first meeting?

No. That had happened in September.

First date?

No. That had happened in March.

First kiss?

No way! Jimmy Bergstrom's legendary spin-the-bottle party had taken place in January.

The first time she and Doug had made love?

No, again. That had happened on a starlit night in June.

The last time they'd made love?

No. Absolutely not. Absolutely...positively...not.

Amy shifted uneasily, causing the lace-trimmed hem of her slip to ride up her thigh. May 16 must have *some* significance for her and Doug! A man didn't send a dozen roses to his ex-wife on impulse. Especially not a man like Douglas Maxwell Browne. In all the time she'd known him—and their relationship dated back to Mrs. Marchini's fourth-grade class—he'd always had a reason for everything he'd done. His purposefulness was one of the things that made him so attractive to her.

One of the many, many things.

So why had he done this?

Amy booted the appointment book off the bed. She just didn't know.

A part of her wished she could add that she just didn't care, either, but she couldn't. She did care. She cared desperately.

Closing her eyes, Amy let her head droop forward. Slowly she rotated it to the right, then to the left. Her neck and shoulders were tied up with tension, like some maniacal Girl Scout had been using her muscles to practice making hitch knots.

Lord, she was tired! She'd been dragging around like a wet dishrag for months. Ms. High-octane Energy was operating on an empty fuel tank and she was unhappily aware that people were starting to notice.

Try to relax, her doctor had suggested over a month ago.

Take a vacation, her boss, Charles Rowand, had ordered only two days before.

Try to relax? Take a vacation! Hah! She had work to do. Work.

Amy opened her eyes and stared at Doug's roses.

It was roughly twenty blocks from Doug's office to the hotel where Amy was staying. Doug decided to walk the distance. He needed the exercise.

He also needed the time to rehearse what he was going to say and how he was going to say it.

He made the trek at a brisk, aerobically beneficial pace. Yet he was honest enough with himself to admit that this physical exertion had very little to do with the way his pulse was racing when he arrived at his destination.

The lavishly appointed hotel lobby was bustling with people. Doug threaded his way through the throng to the small alcove where the house phones were located.

"Operator. Good evening. May I help you?"

"Yes, thank you. I'd like to be connected with Ms. Amy Hilliard's room. That's H-I-double L-I-A-R-D."

"Certainly, sir. One moment."

Doug spent that "one moment" holding his breath and debating with himself.

One ring.

I should have called from the office.

Two rings.

No, this is the way to do it.

Three rings.

God, what if she's gone out?

Four—

"Mmmm...h'lo?"

The voice on the other end was like cashmere: soft, sensual and slightly fuzzy. The tone and texture of it sent a shaft of heat arrowing through Doug's body. He exhaled in a rush.

Obviously Amy had been asleep. Doug was intimately familiar with the voluptuously vulnerable way she sounded when she first woke up. He'd always found it very arousing. Damned near irresistible, in fact.

Doug gripped the receiver. "Amy?" he asked after a second or two.

"D-Doug?"

It was impossible for him to catalogue all the emotions he heard woven into that single, uncertain syllable. "Yes," he confirmed simply.

"Doug?" she repeated. He could hear her shifting around, sitting up. He could imagine her combing her slender fingers through her chin-length hair, trying to order her appearance along with her thoughts. She was probably frowning a little, too, with brows drawn together to create a delicate pleat in the fair skin above her nose.

"Yes. *Doug*. I woke you, didn't I?" He knew she'd fib. She always did.

"Um...no. No, of course not. It's—ah—barely nine. I was just..."

There was an awkward pause. Doug wondered if Amy was nibbling on her lower lip. That particular nervous mannerism of hers had started driving him nuts shortly after they'd exchanged their first real kiss. Oh, he'd noticed her doing it *before* that first kiss, of course, and found himself oddly intrigued. But it wasn't until *after* that he'd really been affected.

It had happened in mid-January of the year they'd been in seventh grade. Doug remembered he'd glanced over at Amy during a math exam about a week after Jimmy Bergstrom's memorable boy-girl bash and suddenly...whammo! The sight of white teeth worrying soft, petal-pink flesh had thrown his body into hormonal overdrive. He'd squirmed through the remainder of the test—scoring a miserable seventy-six to Amy's ninety-six—in a physical state that had been as excruciating as it was embarrassing.

Doug shifted his weight, conscious that the line between adolescence and adulthood was not as firmly drawn as most people liked to think.

"Doug?" Amy's voice was smoother than before, but there were currents of emotion eddying beneath the surface.

"I'm here, Amy."

" 'Here'...where?"

"What?"

"Where are you, Doug?"

"Downstairs."

"H-here? I mean—at this hotel?"

"Yes."

"Oh."

Another pause. Doug wiped the palm of his left hand against the leg of his trousers. This was proving to be more nerve racking than he'd expected.

"I thought we might have a quick drink at the bar," he said finally.

"Together?" The question wasn't coy...exactly. It held a little confusion and a lot of caution.

"Together would be nice," Doug responded. "Unless you'd rather sit at separate tables?"

A breathy sound of amusement—not quite a laugh—teased his ear. "Can you give me a few minutes?"

Doug knew he'd give her all the time he had.

"I'll be waiting for you," he promised.

Amy jabbed impatiently at the elevator call button. She tapped the toe of one calfskin pump against the carpeted floor and flicked a microscopic piece of lint off the cuff of her tobacco-brown linen jacket.

She looked awful. No ifs, ands or buts about it. She looked just plain awful and she knew it. She *felt* it. She could only imagine what Doug was going to think when he saw her.

Amy was acutely aware that she was seldom at her best after a long flight. Spending hours cooped up in some tin can of a jet plane always left her rumpled in body and spirit. The unplanned nap she had somehow drifted into when she was supposed to be preparing for tomorrow's meeting had only compounded the usual problems.

A discreet chime announced the arrival of the elevator. The door slid open to reveal an empty car. Amy stepped in and pressed LOBBY. The door hissed shut. The elevator started to descend.

Amy glanced down and adjusted the oversized carnelian-and-gold pin on the lapel of her jacket, then fiddled with the surplice neckline of her ivory silk blouse. This fiddling led to the discovery that her slim linen skirt had gotten twisted around. She shifted it back into alignment, uncomfortably conscious that the garment which had been tailored to a perfect fit when she'd worn it in Tokyo just a month-and-a-half ago was now a size too large.

Tokyo.

A frisson of emotion shivered through Amy's system as she suddenly recalled her predawn anxiety attack and the near frantic phone call it had provoked. Not that there'd been any real significance to the episode. Unless, of course, she chose to include it with the other unsettling indicators of how badly stressed-out she seemed to be these days.

And yet the memory of those first panicky moments in the dark still haunted her. Those few seconds of feeling alone, utterly alone, seemed to have been seared into her soul.

Doug had phoned her back a couple of days after she'd tried to reach him. He'd never managed to contact her directly. Instead he'd ended up leaving a message with her secretary, and another one on her machine at home. It was the same story when she'd attempted to return his calls. She'd talked to his secretary and to his answering machine rather more briefly, but never to him.

Maybe *that* was why hearing his voice on the other end of the telephone line a few minutes before had shaken her so completely. For an instant or two she'd thought she must be dreaming. Heaven knew, dreaming about Doug was something she'd been doing with disconcerting regularity since their divorce! Yet even when she'd accepted the fact that she was awake and the call was real, the situation had seemed flavored with something very like fantasy.

Amy knew she'd mentioned this trip to New York in the last message she'd left for Doug. There was nothing unusual about that. While she and Doug were no longer husband and wife, they were still friends...after a fashion. And they kept in touch...in a way. But she'd certainly never expected—

Or had she?

Amy stiffened, her fingers tightening around her small leather clutch bag.

Face it, she ordered herself. Face the truth before you face him.

All right, then. No. She hadn't expected to see Doug on this trip. But she had hoped. She had hoped quite a lot.

The last time Doug and she had been together had been roughly four months before. Their paths had crossed, purely by accident, in Chicago. They'd both been there on business and they'd been staying at the same hotel.

They'd had a drink together.

They'd had dinner together.

They'd gone to bed together.

The next morning, they'd kissed goodbye and gone their separate ways.

Amy thought she'd handled the...ah...interlude? One-night stand? Episode of temporary insanity? Whatever, she thought she'd handled it very maturely. She'd wanted him. He'd wanted her. Those wants had been pleasurably fulfilled. But there'd been no pledges made, no promises offered. There'd been no romantic frills like—

Blush-pink roses.

Amy's heart plummeted in the same split second the elevator stopped at the lobby.

Oh, God! she thought despairingly as the door slid open. She hadn't even *mentioned* the roses when Doug had called!

The elevator door opened. Amy stepped out.

Doug consulted his watch. Exactly fourteen minutes and twenty-three seconds had elapsed since the end of his conversation with Amy.

He smoothed his palm against dark hair. He brushed a tiny smudge off his gray jacket. He straightened his tie.

He did *not* look downward to check his fly. He'd already done that several times, and he was aware that he'd caught the attention of a man he suspected was part of the hotel's plainclothes-security force because of it. Doug didn't relish the thought of trying to explain that he was not some kind of pervert—just a man eager to see his ex-wife.

He checked his watch again. Fourteen minutes and fifty-eight seconds.

Doug inhaled slowly, fighting down the impatience that had chewed at him for most of his adult life. He expelled his breath with controlled deliberation.

You said you'd wait, he reminded himself. So—wait!

Doug thrust his hands deep into his pants pockets and rocked back on his heels.

He was standing off to the right of the bank of elevators that would bring Amy down to him. He'd staked out his vantage point carefully. For reasons he couldn't fully explain, it seemed important that he see Amy before she saw him. Maybe it had something to do with the changes he'd undergone in the past six weeks. Doug wasn't sure. He only knew that he wanted—no, *needed* a few moments of being able to watch Amy while she was unaware of his scrutiny.

Then, suddenly, what he wanted—*needed*—was given to him.

Amy Anne Hilliard was not the most beautiful woman Doug had ever seen. But there was an aura about her that made him catch his breath each time he laid eyes on her.

It made him catch his breath this time, too. Yet something was different. Very different.

The hair that could gleam like a new penny in the sun was less glossy than Doug remembered. The fair-skinned, fine-boned face looked pale and angular—all cheekbones and eyes. Beneath the impeccable layers of dress-for-success clothing, the appealingly slim body had dwindled to reed-like thinness.

The obvious signs of stress and strain made Doug ache. They also made him angry. If Amy had been within touching distance, he would have been torn between the desire to sweep her into his arms and hold her safe and the impulse to grab her by the shoulders and shake some sense into her.

Amy, Amy, Doug thought. What's happened to you?

He started toward her.

A heartbeat later, Amy turned her head and spotted him.

Douglas Maxwell Browne was not the most handsome man Amy had ever seen. But there was an aura about him that made her catch her breath each time she laid eyes on him.

It made her catch her breath this time, too. Yet something was different. Very different.

Even at a distance, Amy could see an unfamiliar frosting of silver on the dark hair at Doug's temples. The lines on his strongly molded face, especially the ones that bracketed his mobile mouth, were more deeply etched than she remembered. He appeared a good ten pounds thinner beneath his immaculately tailored gray suit, too, his six-foot-tall body planed down like an endurance athlete's.

Doug looked older than he had four months ago. But he *seemed* younger. He'd been wound up tighter than a watch spring when they'd been together in Chicago. Now he projected a quality of energy and openness that reminded Amy with piercing sweetness of what they'd had and what they'd lost.

Doug . . . Doug, she thought. What's happened to you?

She started toward him.

Somehow, they managed to meet each other halfway.

There was so much Doug wanted to say, so much he wanted to pour out in the first few seconds after he reached her. What came out was: "Hello, Amy."

There was so much Amy wanted to say, so much she wanted to pour out in the first few seconds after she reached him. What came out was: "Hello, Doug."

A pause. Amy looked right, left . . . up, down. She felt the awkward little smile she had plastered on her lips flicker on and off like the electricity service in some Third World country.

Finally she lifted her hazel eyes to gaze into Doug's thick-lashed, deep blue ones. She had to tilt her head back to do so. Even wearing heels, she only came up to her ex-husband's stubborn chin.

"You look . . . wonderful," she blurted out, startling herself and, to judge by the way his brows shot up, Doug as well.

"You look . . . tired," he countered quietly, then stroked the faint hollow beneath her right cheek with the pad of his thumb.

His comment stung her to the quick. His caress stirred her to the core. Amy shied instantly and instinctively from both responses.

"Well, gee, thanks," she retorted. It was one thing for her to think her appearance was far below par. It was entirely another to have him confirm the grim fact to her face!

Doug saw her dismay and was disturbed by it; yet he couldn't bring himself to regret the truth or the touch. "What did you expect from your ex-husband?" he queried lightly.

For an instant, Amy was tempted to be sarcastic. But the expression she glimpsed in the depths of Doug's eyes blunted the edge of the cutting remark that trembled on the tip of her tongue.

After a moment, she gave a little shrug. "Alimony?" she suggested, carefully matching his previous tone.

"Not you," Doug said. The issue of money, like everything else about their divorce, had been amicably settled. He'd kept his. She'd kept hers. They'd split the remainder right down the middle.

"Well . . ." Amy moistened her top lip with the tip of her tongue. She glanced away for a second, then looked back up at him. "I certainly didn't expect blush-pink roses," she said frankly.

"No?" It was impossible to get a fix on his tone.

"No." Amy paused, waiting for Doug to speak. He remained silent. Facing this silence, she found herself strangely reluctant to reveal the emotions his flowers had aroused in her. "They're very beautiful, Doug," she said finally. "Thank you."

"You're welcome."

"But there is . . . one thing."

A hint of wariness entered his gaze. "Yes?"

Amy gestured with her right hand, feeling slightly embarrassed. "I don't have the faintest idea why you sent them," she admitted. "I mean, it's certainly not my birthday. And I don't think it's any of our, um, anniversaries . . . is it?"

"No." Doug shook his head.

"Then why?"

He studied her for several seconds, wondering how to articulate something he was still struggling to explain to himself . . . something he wasn't sure she was ready to hear.

"Doug?" Amy prompted.

He gave her a crooked smile. "Let's just say I was trying to make up for lost time and past mistakes and leave it at that."

Two

Amy was constitutionally incapable of "leaving it at that." She spent the first ten minutes after they sat down at a table in the hotel bar trying—and failing—to get Doug to elaborate on his enigmatic statement. Finally she decided she'd have more luck nailing down a blob of mercury, and she let the matter drop.

The hotel bar was located off the lobby. Decorated with an eye toward the Art Deco era, it created an impression of elegant intimacy leavened with a deft touch of wit.

"Some 'drinks,'" Amy remarked dryly, after the waiter had arrived with their order. She lifted her glass, causing the ice cubes in it to clink together. "Two mineral waters with lime."

"A far cry from those kitchen-sink liqueur extravaganzas you used to order," Doug agreed, picking up his own glass and taking a swallow. Although he'd been a virtual teetotaler during the past month-and-a-half, he didn't feel particularly deprived. Aside from a few beer-swilling binges

during college, he'd always been inclined toward absti-
nence where alcohol was concerned.

Amy rolled her eyes. "Oh, please. Don't remind me." She
fished several almonds from the silver dish of mixed nuts on
the small table that separated them. "I can't believe I once
thought a pousse-café was the height of sophistication." She
popped the almonds in her mouth, then indicated the nut
dish. "Want some?"

Doug shook his head.

"Are you sure?" she questioned, slanting him a tempting look. "I see lots of cashews."

She was, Doug reflected wryly, extremely well-versed
when it came to his weaknesses. Unfortunately, salted
cashews were forbidden fruit—so to speak—to him these
days. So were bacon-cheeseburgers and baked potatoes
slathered with butter and sour cream. He missed such cho-
lesterol-laden goodies a heck of a lot more than Cabernet
and cocktails.

"No, thanks," he refused firmly.

"Such discipline," Amy commented, the green flecks in
her wide-set eyes sparkling. "But, if you insist. None for
you. All for me." She selected and ate two more almonds,
then grimaced, remembering what she'd noticed about the
fit of her skirt a short time before. "I suppose I can use the
calories."

Doug cast a critical eye over what he could see of her
feminine figure and declined to respond. Amy was touchy
about her appearance. It had taken him a long time to recognize that. In fact, he had teased her about the way she
looked for years before he'd realized that she was taking his
banter to heart and being hurt by it. Somehow, she'd never
seemed to hear the compliments he'd hidden behind the
joking criticisms.

She apparently hadn't heard the concern hidden behind
his comment about her looking tired, either.

Amy took a sip of her mineral water, very much aware of
the way Doug's gaze was wandering over the upper part of

her body. She shifted her weight slightly and crossed her legs. "You know," she began, instinctively seeking an impersonal topic, "one of the takeovers I consulted on last year involved a company with a subsidiary distillery operation. Everybody kept complaining that baby boomers are ruining the booze industry."

Doug's mouth twisted at Amy's characteristic retreat into a business-related subject. "Well, I don't think the IRS cuts on business-entertainment deductions have helped much, either," he observed.

"No more three-martini lunches."

"Do you actually know anyone who drinks martinis?"

"Besides James Bond and my father?"

The quirk of his lips became a quick smile. "Yeah."

"Nope." She laughed softly.

Doug leaned back in his chair, savoring the rippling sound of her humor.

"How is your dad these days?" he asked. Amy's mother had died when she was eleven. She'd been a quiet woman and Doug hadn't known her very well, but he'd liked her. His feelings about Amy's father were more complicated. While he was willing to give Albert Hilliard credit for being devoted to Amy, he still found him aloof, unbending and judgmental.

Doug supposed the man's age—he was a decade-and-a-half older than his own parents—had something to do with his reaction. Then again, he'd always had the impression that Albert Hilliard's contemporaries didn't like him very much, either. Respect him? Absolutely. Enjoy his company—not often.

"Oh, the same as always," Amy answered with a little shrug. "He's going to stay in Florida until the end of June. I think this may be the last year he comes back up north for the summer."

"He'll probably sell the house, then."

"Mmm. Probably."

"He'll make a fortune if he does," Doug said offhandedly. "Our former stamping grounds are in the grip of a development boom. There's a major shopping mall going up. Plus a new office complex. And there's going to be a housing subdivision on what used to be the Peterson farm. Real-estate prices are heading for the roof."

"Oh, really?" Even though Amy was aware that Doug's parents and one of his three older brothers still lived in upstate New York, she was surprised by how well informed he seemed to be about what was happening in their old hometown. "I hadn't realized."

Doug saw the sudden sharpening in Amy's gaze and knew he'd come close to saying too much. His ex-wife was a great many things, but slow on the uptake wasn't one of them. "I wouldn't have realized, either, if I hadn't been back recently," he explained.

"You went to see your parents?"

He hesitated for a fraction of a second. Careful, he cautioned himself. "Partly."

"Is everything all right?" Amy asked anxiously, sensing Doug was holding something back. Her concern was genuine. She liked Beth and Lawrence Browne very much.

"Everything's just fine, Amy," Doug assured her. He took a swallow of his mineral water. "My folks are terrific. Actually, I went upstate to close a deal on some property. A house. I decided I needed a place where I can...get away from it all." It wasn't a lie. It certainly wasn't the whole truth, either. But it was close enough. For now.

"Get away from it all?" Amy echoed disbelievingly. "*You?* The man who has a cellular phone in his briefcase and a fax machine in his co-op?"

Amy wasn't being sarcastic. She was simply stating the facts as she knew them. Doug realized that. But her characterization still stung.

She's talking about what I was, he thought. Not what I am...what I want to be.

Amy saw Doug's expression harden. Obviously he hadn't liked what she'd said. "Doug—"

"How did you know about my Fax machine?" he interrupted. Doug remembered finding the thing on when he'd come home from the hospital. Although it had run out of paper days before, it had still been beeping mindlessly, signaling a continuous flow of urgent communications.

Urgent, hah! He'd skimmed through the stuff that had fed in during his absence, then thrown it—and the damned Fax machine—into the trash.

"You told me about it," Amy answered. "The last time we…" She met his eyes for an instant, then looked down at the table. Her lowered lashes cast small, crescent-shaped shadows on her cheeks. "You told me in Chicago."

"Ah. Chicago."

Without warning, the floodgates of memory opened inside Doug.

The yielding sweetness of Amy's mouth…the faintly salty flavor of her perspiration-slick skin. He could *taste* both. The husky whispers of wanting…the throaty cries of pleasure as those wants were ecstatically fulfilled. He could *hear* both. The wild and wondering expression on her flushed face as he came into her, joining their bodies in elemental intimacy. Yes, yes—he could *see* it.

And the feel of her. The press of her small, taut-peaked breasts against his naked chest. The rake of her nails down his back. The hot-satin tightness of her—

Stop it! he ordered himself, sucking in a deep breath. The air seemed to burn as he dragged it into his lungs. Doug picked up his glass and drained the remainder of his mineral water. It cooled him down a bit, but not enough. He was acutely aware that it would have been more effective to dump the icy beverage in his lap.

"Doug?" Amy asked, watching him closely. His eyes had gone midnight-dark. His lightly tanned skin was pulled taut against the strong bones of his face. She could read the subtle signs of physical stress in his body—a body which, through years of intimate exploration, she knew as well as her own.

Amy shifted, moistening her suddenly dry lips with a lick of her tongue. Feminine awareness stirred deep within her, sending a quicksilver message skittering through her nervous system.

"Doug?" she repeated.

Doug took another deep breath. He set his glass down on the table. "Sorry," he apologized.

"For what?"

One corner of his mouth twisted. "Whatever." He gestured as though trying to pluck a reason out of the air. "Chicago, maybe."

"You're sorry about Chicago?" Amy focused on the expressive movement of his hands. Quick, clever hands, with long, lean fingers. She remembered when one of those fingers had worn a simple gold band. A gold band she had slipped carefully into place on the day they had each pledged to love, honor and cherish each other until death did them part.

She remembered the feel of those fingers during the night following that day. She remembered them teasing her... testing her... *touching* her...

Damn him! She couldn't be indifferent to her ex-husband even if she wanted to! And no matter how hard she tried to persuade herself that she *did* want to, Amy knew she didn't. Doug was part of her. He always would be.

Doug looked across the table, seeing the hurt and anger that clouded his ex-wife's changeable gray-green eyes. Her lower lip trembled for an instant. She caught it between her teeth, as though trying to still the telltale quiver.

Damn her! Amy got to him in every way a woman could get to a man, and then some. She was imprinted on every cell of his brain and body. He hadn't intended to say a word about Chicago. Not now. Not tonight. And yet within minutes of seeing her again...

Was he sorry for what had happened in Chicago?

No!

Yes.

Oh, hell. Doug didn't know. He just plain didn't know anymore. In fact, he'd probably never known. What had happened between them in Chicago had been one of the best—and one of the worst—experiences of his life. He'd relived it, and regretted it, more times than he could count.

"Are *you* sorry about Chicago, Amy?" he questioned softly.

She went as pale as skim milk, the powdered blusher on her cheeks standing out like a peach-pink bruise. "No!" she denied vehemently.

Doug remained silent, watching her very steadily.

Amy sustained his gaze for nearly fifteen seconds, then dropped her eyes. "Yes," she contradicted herself finally. Her eyes bounced back to his. "I mean—"

Words and feelings refused to mesh. Amy's mouth opened and closed several times, but nothing came out. She looked down again. A pecan had fallen out of the nut dish. Needing some kind of vent for the frustration welling up inside her, Amy flicked the nut with the tip of her index finger and sent it flying off the table. She would have felt better if she had been able to chuck the whole bowl of salted snacks through a plate-glass window.

"Amy?"

Reluctantly, she lifted her eyes to her ex-husband's once more. "I don't know if I'm sorry or not," she told him at last. "Sometimes I . . . but then . . . I mean—" She heaved a heavy sigh and shook her head. "Oh, I don't know. I'm so . . . so . . ."

Confused? Tired? Afraid? A host of adjectives presented themselves. Amy instinctively rejected them all. Not because they weren't accurate. Quite the contrary. But to offer any of those accurate adjectives would force her to offer explanations for them, as well, and she wasn't ready to do that. Not now. Not tonight. Not . . . to Doug.

"I just plain don't know anymore," she finished. There was a fractional pause, then she summoned up a crooked smile. "Uh-oh." She gave an embarrassed little laugh, trying to distance herself from the admission she'd just made. "Yuppie angst. I guess I've got the baby-boomer blues."

For a moment, Doug was tempted to push her. He wanted to hold her words up to her like a mirror and demand: "Don't you see what you're doing to yourself?" But he held back. Amy was one of the strongest women—no, one of the strongest *people*—he'd ever known. Yet there was a fragility about her this evening that she'd never shown him before. It disturbed him more than a little. And until he understood the reasons for it, he knew he had to be very careful. After all, he was still in the process of putting his own life back together. He was scarcely ready to start rearranging the pieces of somebody else's!

But, Lord, the temptation was very strong.

"To tell the truth, it sounds as though you're the one who should be thinking about getting away from it all," he said at last.

"What?" Amy questioned, thrown off balance by this remark. Then she realized that Doug was picking up an earlier thread in their conversation. "Oh. Well. Yes. I guess."

"Is that, 'yes,' you guess you *sound* like you should be thinking about getting away from it, or 'yes,' you guess you *are* thinking about it?" Doug inquired, lifting a brow.

Amy ran the tip of one finger around the rim of her glass, wondering if Doug realized that she found this topic only marginally less troubling than the previous one. She decided he probably did. There were times when her ex-husband seemed to be able to read her innermost emotions as if they'd been emblazoned on a highway billboard.

"I guess I *am* thinking about it," she said reluctantly, tucking a lock of coppery-brown hair back behind one ear.

Doug leaned forward. "Really?"

Amy could tell she'd surprised him and she took a perverse kind of pleasure in it. Yet she was nettled by the skepticism of his tone, too.

"Yes, really," she told him flatly.

He frowned, once again registering her pallor and thinness. He knew the violet-gray shadowing beneath her eyes wasn't smudged mascara. Anxiety touched him with cold, clammy fingers. Dear God, what if she were—

"Is something wrong, Amy?" he asked abruptly.

She couldn't have sat up any more rigidly if he'd skewered her with a broomstick.

"No. Of course not!" The rejection of the possibility was as quick as it was categorical.

"Then—"

"I tell you I'm thinking about taking some time off from work, and you want to know if something's wrong? Why should something be wrong, Doug? Isn't it normal for people to think about taking time off?" Amy realized she was becoming a bit shrill. She took a deep breath. "What do you think I am, anyway?" she demanded in a more moderate tone.

It was a loaded question, Doug reflected. That the situation between them was primed and ready to blow was obvious. He had the distinct impression that his next words would either detonate things . . . or defuse them.

"What do I think you are?" he echoed slowly. "Hmm. Well—how about a woman who has a cellular phone in her briefcase and a fax machine at home."

Amy's eyes widened and her mouth dropped open. For one horrible moment, Doug was sure he'd made an awful mistake. Then to his profound relief, she started to laugh. The sound came bubbling up out of her like foam out of a shaken champagne bottle.

"Touché," she finally managed to say.

Doug inclined his dark head in acknowledgement.

Amy picked up her glass with a not quite steady hand and took a deep gulp. A piece of ice slipped between her lips. "Mmmee onnee 'hing—" she began.

"Excuse me?"

Grimacing, Amy bit down on the ice and shattered it. She swallowed the shards and set the glass back on the table. "The only thing is—" she repeated distinctly "—I don't have a fax machine in my house anymore."

"No?"

She shook her head. "No. Now I have one in my car."

"Are you serious?"

"Of course, I'm serious. Do you think I'd make something like that up?"

"You live in L.A., Amy. I thought they made *everything* up out there."

"Do I detect a note of Manhattan snobbery, Doug?"

"Well, you know what Woody Allen said: 'Who would want to live in a place—'"

"'Where the only cultural advantage is that you can turn right on red?'" Amy felt a twinge of nostalgia. She was the one who'd dragged Doug to the movie in which Woody Allen had made that particular assertion. "Well, somebody *else* once said that New York City is the only place in the world where you can get deliberately run down by a pedestrian."

Doug grinned. "The Quotation Queen strikes again. Now I remember why you were the state's outstanding high-school debater for two years in a row."

The remark was very much in character for him, Amy reflected. Doug had always been proud of her accomplishments. But it had taken her a long time to accept this, and an even longer time to accept the true nature of his teasing comments about her achievements.

Amy wished with all her heart that she'd recognized Doug's humor for what it was—a building up, not a belittling—much, much earlier in their relationship. Because, by the time she finally figured out there was love behind the laughter, he'd all but stopped making jokes.

Oddly enough, when Doug thought about her high-school debating career, he obviously recalled her victories. Yet *her* most vivid memory of that particular extracurricular activity centered on how miserably she'd fared during her first state competition.

Doug had been watching the play of emotion on Amy's face, trying to gauge what she was thinking. He'd seen her smile for a moment or two, her soft lips curving into an expression of luminescent sweetness. Then suddenly the light had vanished from her features . . . like a candle flame snuffed out by a chill wind.

"Amy?" he questioned.

She blinked, then looked at him, her eyes coming back into focus. "I—I'm sorry," she apologized, feeling very vulnerable. "I was . . . remembering."

The admission surprised him. Not *what* she'd said; the fact that she'd said it. "I know how that is," he responded softly.

"Do you?"

He nodded slowly. "Yeah, I do."

There was a brief silence. Amy ate another three almonds, licking at the salt that clung to her fingertips. Doug knew the gesture was an unthinking one, but it affected him like a deliberate effort to seduce. Feeling his blood start to thicken and heat, Doug glanced down at the table in a bid to distract himself. He noticed that the ice in his glass had begun to melt. He drank the inch or so of lukewarm water this process had produced in a single, gulping swallow.

"So, tell me about your time off from work," he invited finally. Amy gave him an odd look, making him wonder whether his voice sounded as strange to her ears as it did to his.

"There's not much to tell," she answered. "I have to take three weeks' vacation."

"Have to?"

"Have to," she confirmed. "My boss, Chaz, has this theory about all work and no play."

"He thinks it makes people extremely successful?"

She laughed briefly. "Not exactly."

"Mmm. When does this vacation of yours start?" The seed of an idea had started to germinate in his brain.

Amy shrugged. She toyed with the brooch on the lapel of her jacket. "I'm not sure," she said after a few seconds. She didn't really want to talk about her 'vacation.' She didn't even want to *think* about it. Three weeks away from her job. What would she do?

She'd go crazy, that's what she'd do.

"You're not sure," Doug repeated without inflection.

"Two, maybe three weeks. As soon as I wrap up the Japanese deal I've been working on. It seems pretty well set in stone at this point. But, still, I can't really be sure of anything until the final papers are signed."

"And before that happens, an earthquake might wipe out Tokyo and you could end up back at square one, right?" he remarked in a perfectly reasonable tone. "That would really put a crimp in your vacation schedule."

Her eyes widened. "What?" she asked, uncertain whether she should be insulted or amused by the scenario he'd just offered.

"You *do* have a tendency to expect the worst, Amy."

"Well, things go wrong sometimes, Doug," she countered a tad stiffly. "I want to be prepared. I think contingency planning is very important."

"Oh, believe me. I know. You shanghaied me into working on the senior prom with you, remember? You were probably the best prom-committee chairperson in the history of high school, but you drove me nuts with all the 'what ifs' you kept dreaming up. My God, Amy! You were ready for anything."

"No, I wasn't," she corrected wryly. "I wasn't ready for a flood."

"A flood," Doug began, then gave her a crooked grin. "Oh. *That*. So, you haven't forgotten my little joke, hmm?"

"Little joke?" she repeated, the edges of each syllable very sharp. "We walked into the gym on prom night and the first thing you said was: 'Where are the lifeboats?'"

"Whoa." Doug shook his head emphatically. "The first thing I said was: 'This place is almost as beautiful as you are.' You blushed. Then I asked where the lifeboats were."

Amy felt her cheeks warm. Doug's memory was accurate. His straightforward compliment about her appearance had caught her completely unaware on that lovely night so many years before. So had the look he'd given her. The look had been young man to young woman, not boy to girl. Before she'd had a chance to recover from her hot-faced, heart-pounding confusion, he'd made his ridiculous remark about lifeboats.

"And then *you* said—" he prompted.

"'What lifeboats?'"

"And I said—"

"'What if there's a flood? Shouldn't we have lifeboats?'"

They spoke the words simultaneously, then laughed together.

"I wanted to brain you for that, Doug," Amy said after a few seconds.

"You wanted to brain me after you realized I was jerking your chain. But you can't tell me you didn't spend at least ten seconds seriously trying to figure out where you could get a last-minute deal on rented lifeboats."

He was right, of course.

"Not that I don't believe you couldn't have come up with lifeboats if we'd really needed them," he added candidly.

Amy was taken aback by the admiration she thought she heard embroidering the edges of this assertion. "Thank you," she responded with an awkward little dip of her head.

"You're welcome," he returned simply.

Their conversation drifted pleasantly for the next half hour or so. Looking back later, it seemed to Amy that they'd both decided it would be wiser to stick to relatively impersonal topics. There were no awkward silences, no abrupt changes of subjects. Their wide-ranging chitchat was very smooth and essentially superficial.

Just about the time they'd finished a second round of mineral waters, Amy began to yawn.

"Ahmmm." She tried to force the sound back into her mouth with her hand. It wouldn't fit. "Sorry," she said to Doug, then stole a swift glance at her watch. She blinked, startled by the time she thought she read. No. It couldn't be this late.

She took another look. Good Lord, it was!

"Doug—" she began.

"I know," he cut her off easily. "It's late. I apologize. I invited you for a quick drink."

"No. No. It's oka-aaahhhmmf." The yawn was a long one. "It's okay," Amy finally got out. "I'm just a little tired. You know how I am when I travel across more than one time zone."

"And you've probably got a morning meeting, right?"

She smiled ruefully. "The requisite power breakfast."

"Mmm. To tell the truth, I've got to be up and at 'em early, too." Reaching for his wallet, he signaled their waiter.

They left as soon as their tab was settled. As they moved toward the bar's exit, Doug took Amy's arm. Although the contact was light, she was very conscious of his touch. The warmth of his fingers seemed to penetrate straight through her jacket and blouse.

"Well," he said once they'd reached the bank of elevators in the lobby. He released her arm and pressed the call button.

"Well," Amy responded, looking up at him. They were standing close enough so she could smell his scent—a hint of natural male musk mixed with the faint citrus tang of an expensive after-shave.

Doug's gaze tracked from her wide eyes to her slightly parted lips, then slid briefly down the smooth line of her throat before reversing course. He was struck once again by how fragile his ex-wife seemed. And not just in a physical sense, either. She struck him as being both emotionally wound up *and* worn down.

"Are you busy tomorrow night?" he asked.

Amy hesitated. "I, well, actually, I was planning to catch an evening flight back to L.A."

"Would you consider planning to have dinner with me instead?"

Amy caught her breath. She felt her heart miss a beat. No. *Two* beats. Her mind skipped back twice that many months.

Chicago.

They'd had a drink together.

They'd had dinner together.

And then, they'd gone to bed.

"*Just* dinner," Doug promised gently.

It took Amy a very painful split second to realize that the slight but unmistakable emphasis he'd placed on the adjective was meant to reassure—not reject. With that realization came a sudden flash of insight: whether or not Doug was sorry about what had happened between them in Chicago, he remembered it as vividly as she did. She could see echoes of their encounter in the depths of his blue eyes and in the throbbing pulse of the vein in his right temple.

Amy exhaled slowly.

There were a lot of reasons for her to say no to Doug's invitation. Good reasons. Solid, sensible reasons.

There were a lot of reasons for her to say yes to it, too. Not bad reasons, exactly. But not solid or sensible ones, either.

In the end, only one reason mattered. She *wanted* to accept.

So she did.

"Shall we meet somewhere?" she suggested.

Doug shook his head. "No. I'll pick you up here at the hotel at—oh, say, eight?"

"All right," Amy agreed after a second. "I—we'll probably need reservations."

"I'll make the necessary arrangements, Amy."

She bridled just a little at her ex-husband's take-charge manner. "You have somewhere in mind, then?"

"Mmm-hmm." Amy saw an odd expression flicker across his face.

"Am I supposed to guess?" she inquired.

Doug's mouth curved into a crooked smile. Lifting his right hand, he stroked the knuckle of one finger down the line of her cheek. He watched her lips part and felt a tiny tremor of response run through her.

"No, Amy," he told her. "You're supposed to be surprised."

Three

———

She was.

"I can't get over the fact that Rossellini's is still open," Amy declared shortly before nine-thirty the following evening. "The last time we were here was—what, Doug? Six years ago?"

She glanced around as she spoke, reacquainting herself with a cheerfully garish interior that obviously owed nothing to the services of a professional decorator.

Nothing's changed, she thought. She continued to let her eyes roam, noting that the evening's diners ranged from a chain-smoking, stubble-chinned loner to a trio of solemnly dressed older men and their well-corseted wives. It's like a time warp, she marveled. Even the people are the same!

Suddenly, Amy caught a glimpse of herself and Doug in one of the gilt-framed mirrors that punctuated the red brick walls. She, in smoke-slate silk by Giorgio Armani. He, in navy pinstripes by someone on Savile Row.

She realized in that instant that her initial assessment had been wrong. Things were not the same. At least two of the people present were very different than they had been the last time they'd entered this place.

"Actually, it's closer to seven years," Doug said, watching the ebb and flow of emotion across his ex-wife's face.

Like Amy, he had been astonished to discover that this particular eatery was still operating. He'd impulsively looked the place up in the telephone directory the previous day, shortly after dispatching the blush-pink roses to Amy's hotel. Sure enough, there it had been: same name, same address, same number.

"Closer to seven?" Amy echoed, giving Doug a skeptical look.

"Around the time you got your first big promotion."

She thought back. He was right. She said as much. "We were living on West End Avenue," she recalled, then laughed. "In the building with the madam."

"I think Cybille preferred the term 'independent businesswoman.'"

Amy laughed lightly and shook her head. Doug watched the silver earrings she was wearing wink against her burnished hair. "Almost seven years! And Signore Rossellini still recognized us when we walked in." She smiled a little as she recalled the open-armed welcome she and Doug had received from the restaurant's proprietor.

"Well, we used to come here a lot," Doug pointed out. By his reckoning, he and Amy had eaten at Rossellini's at least once a month during the early years of their marriage. "The price was right—"

"And so was the pasta," Amy completed. She forked up the final smidgen of the flawlessly prepared clams posillipo that had been presented as their starter. There had been no question of ordering off the menu for this meal. After personally escorting them to a corner table, Signore Rossellini had expansively informed them that his wife would prepare something special for them. "In any case, it's nice to be remembered."

"Well, it's obvious that you're better remembered than I am." He extracted a piece of warm, crusty bread from the basket that had been brought with their appetizer. He tore it in half in a shower of crumbs and handed one chunk to Amy.

"Oh?" She used the bread to mop up some of the rich, tomatoey broth that remained on her plate, then popped it between her lips.

"Clams posillipo is your favorite, not mine."

Amy looked across at his plate. Like hers, it was mounded high with now empty mollusk shells. It took her a few seconds to chew and swallow the bread in her mouth. "Let me guess," she said dryly. "You forced yourself to choke them down so you wouldn't hurt Signora Rossellini's feelings, right?"

"You know me too well." Laughter glinted in his eyes.

"Such gallantry," she applauded. "Or do I mean gluttony?"

Doug grinned. "A little bit of both, I suspect. And speaking of gluttony..." He glanced over her shoulder toward the rear of the restaurant.

"Yes?"

"Here comes the waiter with our main course."

Their entree turned out to be sautéed chunks of unboned chicken mixed with thick slices of green bell peppers and onions. The dish was flavored with enough garlic to keep Count Dracula and most of his vampire kin at bay for at least a week.

"Mmm," Amy sighed blissfully after taking a few bites. "This is wonderful."

"Terrific," Doug concurred, neatly separating a large piece of meat from bone and bisecting it with near surgical precision.

For the second time in as many days, Amy found herself watching her ex-husband's hands. The sure, supple strength of his movements triggered a memory. It was something she hadn't thought about in years.

"You've still got a knack for slicing things up, I see," she remarked.

Doug paused in the act of forking up a piece of chicken. "Excuse me?"

Amy took a sip of red wine, then patted her lips with her napkin. "Junior-year biology."

It took Doug a second to figure out what she was talking about. When he did, he laughed. "Oh, God. Frog Killer Culhane." He ate the bite of meat, then set his fork down. "I saved your 'A' in that class, Amy," he asserted.

"I wouldn't go quite that far," Amy objected.

"Oh, really?" He cocked a brow. "Who did all the dissecting? Despite the fact that we were supposed to split it fifty-fifty. Culhane would have flunked us both if he'd realized what we were doing."

"Well—"

"I should have known you were going soft when you insisted on naming the frog."

Amy sniffed. "Kermit died for science. I thought he deserved a little respect."

"Kermit was a girl, Amy."

"We didn't know that until we dissected him."

"Until I dissected her."

"All right. All right," Amy conceded ungraciously. "I'll give you credit for the cutting."

"Thank you."

"You're welcome. But don't forget: I did all the diagrams. I can only imagine what Mr. Culhane would have said if we'd turned in the ones *you* drew."

"Mine weren't that awful, Amy," he protested.

"They looked like abstract art, Doug."

"Well, if it was good enough for Picasso..."

"Bad abstract art," she amended immediately. "Done in a dark room during an earthquake."

"Ouch!" Doug held up his hands in a gesture of mock-surrender. "Okay. If you insist. I'll admit I wasn't totally responsible for the 'A' you got on the frog dissection."

"The 'A' *we* got," Amy corrected, caught up in the spirit of their banter. "We were partners, remember?"

Everything seemed to stop.

Oh, God. Oh, God, Amy berated herself silently. Why did I have to say that?

Doug picked up his wineglass and took a slow drink. He saw the unhappiness in Amy's gray-green eyes and wanted to ease it. Unfortunately he knew there was no simple panacea for her pain.

Nor for his.

"Yes, Amy," he affirmed quietly. "I remember."

"Doug—"

He silenced her with a quick shake of his head. "It's all right. We *were* partners."

"And now we're . . . ex-partners."

"And friends."

"Friends?"

"I hope so."

Amy looked at Doug for several long moments. This was a man she knew better than any other in the world. Yet something about him was so . . . so *different* than she remembered. She wondered, going cold and still, whether the change she sensed in him was due to another woman.

"Amy?"

She shifted suddenly. He would have told me, she thought with fierce conviction. If he'd found someone new, he would have told me.

"I hope we're friends, too, Doug," she answered.

They traded tales about their professional lives for the rest of the meal. It was only as they found themselves lingering over the espresso and anisette Signore Rossellini had insisted on serving them that Doug broached the subject he'd been mulling over for most of the past twenty-four hours.

"I've been thinking about this vacation of yours," he began.

"You have?" Amy was genuinely surprised. "Why?"

"Because I'm going to be taking a couple of weeks off around the same time you are."

She brushed at her hair. "Oh...really?" She thought she heard about a two-octave difference between the first word and the second.

"Yes. Really." He toyed with his espresso cup, staring down into the dark, aromatic brew it contained like a fortune-teller consulting a particularly enigmatic set of tea leaves. "I'm planning to go upstate."

Amy wasn't certain what she'd expected Doug to say, but she knew that wasn't it. "You—you're going home?" She might have been talking about Mars rather than a place not too many miles up the New York State Thruway from Saratoga Springs.

The shape of Doug's mouth altered, forming something that wasn't quite a smile. "So to speak." He let a few seconds go by, then raised his eyes to meet Amy's. "I think you should come, too."

Amy gaped. "Wh-what?" she managed to get out.

Doug repeated himself.

"But—" What he was suggesting was crazy! She hadn't been back to their hometown in more than three—no, in more than *four* years.

"Look." Doug leaned forward slightly, his expression intent. "You said you don't have a choice about taking this time off. Fine. But you *do* have a choice about how you spend it. You know how beautiful it is up around the Adirondacks this time of year. There's plenty of peace and quiet. And with your father still in Florida, you've got the perfect place to stay. You can do what you like, when you like."

Amy averted her gaze and worried her lower lip with her teeth for a second or two. Then she asked, "And you?"

"The place I've bought—the one I mentioned yesterday—needs some work, but it's livable. I'll be around."

"I see," Amy responded, but she was not at all sure she did.

"What's the problem?" he questioned, keeping his tone light. "You don't think the town's big enough for the two of us?"

That brought her eyes back to his face. She gave him a sharp look. Then, unable to help herself, she laughed. "No, of course not."

"Well, then?" His tone was still light.

Amy shifted. "This is very sudden, Doug," she stalled.

"You have..." He hesitated, aware of a knotting in his stomach. "You have commitments?" Amy hadn't been involved with anyone four months ago. Of that, Doug was certain. She never would have made love with him if she had been. But just because his ex-wife had been unattached then didn't mean she was unattached now.

Amy understood what her ex-husband was asking and, oddly, she didn't resent the prying. She waited several moments, then shook her head once. No, she thought. No commitments. No affairs. No flings. And if she was honest...no inclination.

No time, either. But that was another issue.

Doug realized he had been holding his breath. He exhaled slowly. "So?" he prompted.

"So—" Amy gestured, torn by a dozen contradictory emotions.

Doug reached across the table and gathered Amy's hands into his own. It was the first time he'd touched her since they'd entered the restaurant. It was not the first time he'd wanted to.

"No strings, Amy," he said quietly.

Amy had to fight to keep her hands from trembling within the warmly familiar enclosure of his palms. She could do nothing to control the sudden acceleration of her pulse. It went from fast trot to flat-out gallop in the space of a single second.

"What about loose ends?" she eventually inquired.

The curving of Doug's lips acknowledged the ties that had bound them together for most of their lives. "We do have a few of those, don't we."

"More than a few, Doug."

"Maybe..." He paused, his thumbs moving gently, very gently, against her wrists. "Maybe we should spend some time together tying them up."

Neither of them spoke for about thirty seconds. Finally, Amy made a small movement of withdrawal. "No strings?" she asked.

Doug released her hands immediately. "No strings," he affirmed. "Just lots of fresh air. Maybe a little wholesome fun. And... friendship."

She swallowed. "Sounds like old times."

"Something like that."

Amy's gaze strayed briefly to the mirror she'd noticed earlier. "We can't turn back the clock, Doug."

"I know that, Amy." Despite the roses he had sent the day before and the restaurant he had chosen tonight, Doug didn't want to recapture the past. His goal was to reclaim the future—the future that he and the first and only woman he'd ever loved had thrown away without realizing what they were doing.

Another pause. Shorter than the previous one. It ended when Amy made up her mind. Attuned to every nuance of her expression, Doug sensed the instant her decision was made. He also sensed exactly what that decision was. "You'll come?" he asked.

"I'll come," she answered. Then after a few seconds she offered him a slow, sweet smile.

Later Doug told himself that this had been the moment he should have told Amy the truth. But something deep inside him—something he couldn't or wouldn't put a name to—

kept him from speaking. It stopped him from saying the things he knew needed to be said.

The moment slipped by and was irrevocably lost.

Doug tried to soothe the uneasiness in his soul with the thought that the smile he gave his ex-wife in exchange for her own was honest, even though the silence he kept wasn't.

Amy and Doug came to a halt in front of her hotel room about forty-five minutes later.

"Well, this is it," she announced unnecessarily.

"Ten-sixty-six," he observed, noting the number on the door. "A good year for Normans."

"What? Oh. William the Conqueror and the Battle of Hastings."

"World History 101. The class where I perfected the fine art of sleeping with my eyes open."

It was typical of Doug, Amy thought, to make it sound as though he'd spent the entire course goofing off. "You aced the final, as I recall."

"So did you," he countered. "Then again, you aced just about everything you took at Syracuse."

Amy said nothing. She'd known the standards she'd been expected to achieve in college and she'd achieved them.

Achieved *most* of them, she amended after a moment. She'd been good. But she hadn't been good enough.

"Amy?"

The stroke of Doug's fingertips accompanied the sound of his voice. A white-hot shiver went through Amy. "Y-yes?" she asked, the word catching in her throat.

"Are you okay?" He brushed her cheek again, even more lightly than the first time. Her skin was very soft and her changeable eyes had gone more gray than green. Doug could see emotions swirling through them like smoke on a breeze.

"Yes, I'm fine." Amy nodded quickly. She had a sudden, almost desperate urge to turn her face into the curve of his palm. She resisted it. "I just have a lot on my mind."

Doug lifted his hand away from her cheek and brought it back down to his side. "I see." His fingers curled inward and clenched. "Are you regretting you said yes to me earlier?"

She blinked. "What?"

"I'm talking about your saying yes to my idea about your vacation," he elaborated. "Are you having second thoughts about that?"

She stared at him, then shook her head. "No," she answered, surprising herself a little. Maybe she would have second, third and fourth thoughts in the morning, but not tonight. Not while she was with him. "No. I'm not."

"Are you sure?" A pang of guilt lanced through him. "Look, Amy, if I maneuvered you—" He stopped. Oh, hell. If he'd maneuvered her, he'd done exactly what he'd intended and he damned well knew it! "What I mean is—"

Amy stopped the flow of his words by the simple expedient of placing one of her hands against the front of his jacket. She heard Doug catch his breath, felt his lean body tense. She derived an unsettling surge of feminine satisfaction from the knowledge that her touch affected him so strongly.

Lifting her chin, she looked her ex-husband squarely in the face. "I'm a thirty-five-year-old woman, Doug," she told him. "I'm not a...a shopping cart. Nobody maneuvers me." Her chin went up another notch. "Not even you."

"Amy—"

"Of course," she went on, adopting a wry tone, "given that you're bigger and stronger than I am, you *could* probably push me around a little."

The silence that fell might have lasted more than a minute or less than a moment. Amy never had any way of calculating. Hazel eyes locked with dark blue ones in elemental communication, and time was temporarily obliterated.

The silence ended when Doug made a sound that could have been a laugh.

"Push you around?" he echoed, lifting his brows in disbelief. "Sweetheart, I have six inches and at least sixty pounds on you, but I wouldn't even want to try."

And then Doug did something he knew he shouldn't do. Something he'd promised himself—and her, in a way—he *wouldn't* do. Something he was honest enough to admit he'd been wanting to do ever since he'd seen Amy step out of the hotel elevator and into the lobby more than twenty-four hours before.

Slowly, deliberately, he bent his head and kissed his ex-wife full on the mouth.

Amy's lips had parted at Doug's unexpected use of the endearment. They parted even further when he covered them with his own. Her lashes fluttered down. Her head tilted back as the muscles of her neck went as pliant as melting wax.

She felt Doug's arms circle her waist. He pulled her close against him. The press of his palm and fingers was possessive, making an unspoken but unmistakable claim on her body.

Amy went up on tiptoe, her stockinged heels rising out of her black lizard pumps. She arched against Doug, instinctively seeking the fit that had always existed for them, even in the midst of the awkwardness and inexperience of their first time together.

Her right arm was trapped between their bodies for a moment, but she shifted so she could move it upward...upward to Doug's shoulder and then around his neck. She brought her left arm up, too, fingers tunneling into the dark, thick hair at the back of his head.

Amy whimpered softly as Doug deepened the kiss. The stroke of his tongue was bold, evoking an even more intimate joining. She slid her tongue against his, teasing, tempting.

Doug tightened his hold and felt Amy quiver beneath the sleek, expensive silk of her sleek, expensive dress. He let one hand flow up the supple line of her back. Amy twisted against him. He wove his fingers into the soft tangle of her hair. He inhaled, his nostrils filling with the scent of her perfumed skin.

He wanted her. Oh, God, how he wanted her.

Desire thudded in Doug's brain and bloodstream.

It was beating. Like his heart.

Pounding. Like his heart.

Hammering. Like his—

No. No. Not again. Not now!

Amy could never clearly recall what happened during the next few moments. She only knew that at the end of them, she was no longer in Doug's arms.

"D-Doug?" She had to brace her hand against a wall to keep from staggering.

The sound of his breathing was harsh. The sound of his voice, when he finally spoke, was anything but. "Amy." He paused to take another breath. "We have to stop."

"Stop?" Shock steadied legs that had been as wobbly as unset gelatin. She stared at Doug, trying to make sense of his words . . . of his expression . . . of *something.*

The unsettled pattern of his breathing slowed and smoothed. There was a look in his midnight-blue eyes that Amy couldn't begin to describe, let alone decipher. He turned his head slightly. She could see a vein pulsing wildly in his temple.

"Doug!"

"We're in the middle of a hotel hallway, Amy," he said huskily.

The sentence could have been spoken in Urdu for all the luck her brain had sorting out its meaning.

Then abruptly the reality of their situation snapped into focus. Amy realized where she was, and what she had been doing. She made a noise that was somewhere between an embarrassed groan and an appalled giggle. "Oh, God, Doug. I wasn't th-thinking . . ." Her voice trailed off.

He looked at her again. "Neither was I."

Amy stroked her palms against the subtly styled skirt of her dress, drawing on her badly depleted reserves of poise. She eased her weight from one foot to the other, acutely conscious of the strain of her breasts against the fabric of her bra and bodice. She moistened her lips. Finally, fully aware of the implications of what she was about to do, she shifted her gaze toward the door to her room.

After a moment, Doug shook his head.

Amy felt her cheeks flame. "You don't want—"

He put his hands into his trouser pockets. Amy saw the outline of the movement of his fingers clenching and un-clenching and realized with a shock that he was forcing himself not to touch her again.

"I 'want' as much as you do," he informed her tightly.

"Then, why—" She stopped abruptly, suddenly under-standing. She could sum up his reasons in a single word: Chicago.

"You're flying back to L.A. in less than nine hours, sweetheart," he said, confirming the comprehension he saw in her eyes. "I won't go to bed with you tonight knowing I'll have to say goodbye to you tomorrow morning. I did that once before. I don't want to do it again." He waited a mo-ment, then added quietly, "I don't believe you want to do it, either."

Amy was alone when she let herself into her hotel room some three minutes later. Her lips were tingling from the kiss Doug had brushed against them before he'd whispered farewell.

She spent half the night wondering what her ex-husband would have done if he'd known that she would have ripped up her airline ticket if he'd asked her to.

She spent the other half wondering why she'd waited for him to ask, when she could have offered.

Four

In other words," Paul Lansing summed up mildly, "nothing happened." He scribbled a note on the chart he was holding.

"I wouldn't say that," Doug responded irritably. "Can I get dressed now?"

"Oh, sure. I'm finished. You're fine." Lansing made another notation, then gave Doug an owlish look. "So just how far *did* things go between you and Amy last night?"

Doug got off the examination table and picked up his shirt. He yanked the garment on. "Not as far as they went in Chicago," he returned through gritted teeth. While he'd certainly never given Paul Lansing any graphic details about what had happened between him and Amy in the Windy City, he knew the other man was perceptive enough to have drawn some accurate conclusions from the things he *had* said. "Satisfied?"

"More so than you, apparently."

Doug paused, giving his physician—and friend—a sharp look. "Is that a professional observation?"

Lansing seemed untroubled by Doug's contentious manner. "Performance anxiety isn't unusual after a heart attack," he commented after a moment.

"What?"

"Concerns about . . . impotence."

Doug snorted. If he'd been any more *potent* the previous night, he would have broken the zipper on the front of his trousers!

"I didn't ask for this checkup because I was worried about that portion of my anatomy, Paul," he retorted. "Amy and I—we got a little carried away at the end of the evening. In the middle of the excitement, I suddenly started to feel as though my heart was . . . well, what I mean is—"

"You were suddenly afraid you might come and go," the other man stated bluntly.

Doug grimaced, then nodded. "Yes," he admitted. "Crudely put. But yes." He began buttoning up the front of his shirt.

"That kind of apprehension isn't unusual either, Doug," Lansing said matter-of-factly. "Now, I'm certainly not recommending you go out and start working your way through the *Kama Sutra*. But there's nothing in your condition that contraindicates normal sexual relations." He paused, scratching his forehead and clearly weighing his words before he spoke them. "I take it you still haven't said anything to Amy about your heart attack."

Doug tucked his shirt into his trousers. He shook his head.

The other man sighed. "I should have called her. If you hadn't been so insistent—"

"Amy was on the other side of the world when it happened," Doug interrupted.

"And afterward? When you were recovering?"

"Oh, hell, Paul! You know what I went through. I mean, there's nothing like ending up flat on your back in a hospital emergency room to change your perspective on life! And even after I got through the worst of it physically, I was still pretty wobbly emotionally. I didn't—I *couldn't* let Amy see me that way.''

"Ego?"

Doug raked his fingers back through his hair. "As in macho pride? That was probably part of it.''

"And now? You say you want Amy back.''

"Oh, God. Yes.''

"Then you're going to have to tell her the truth, Doug. The *whole* truth. For heaven's sake, man! You're quitting your job. You've bought a house and you're planning to move upstate. You're essentially overhauling your entire existence and you want her to do the same.''

"Dammit!" Doug cut in explosively. "I don't want Amy to change *her* life because of *my* heart attack!" He paused, trying to moderate his emotions, then continued. "Sure, I'm hoping the time we're going to spend together will make her realize that there's more to life than trying to be the big cheese in the rat race. But in the end what she does has to be her decision.''

"I understand.''

"Look, Paul," Doug went on intensely. "I know all the things I need to say to Amy and haven't. I know that if we're going to have another chance together I'm going to have to say them. I came close—" he held up his right hand, thumb and forefinger held a fraction of an inch apart "—this close to telling her yesterday after she agreed to come upstate with me. But I couldn't. I just couldn't. Not right then.''

There was a short, sharp silence. Finally Paul Lansing spoke. "You couldn't tell her you didn't want her to go to L.A. a few years back, either," he recalled quietly.

Doug stiffened. "I knew what that job meant to her," he answered tightly. "She'd worked so damned hard. She deserved it, and more. I couldn't stand in her way. Besides, I thought we could work things out. Sure, I knew it would be tough with her living on one coast and me on the other. We both did. But still . . .''

He fell silent, wrestling with a legion of could, would, and should have beens. He was aware that Paul Lansing was watching him very closely.

''But still what, Doug?'' his friend prompted after several long moments.

Doug looked at him. ''What do you want me to say? That I was afraid of what would've happened if I'd asked Amy to choose between taking the job in L.A. and staying with me in New York? Okay. I'll say it. Deep down in my gut, I was afraid. That's one of the things I've had to face during the past six weeks or so. And I'm afraid now, too. I'm afraid it may be too late for Amy and me.''

The plump brunette sitting opposite Amy froze, a forkful of eggs Benedict halfway to her well-glossed lips.

''What do you mean—if that's all Doug wanted he could have had it three nights ago?'' she demanded after a few seconds, putting down the eating utensil. Her artfully plucked eyebrows arched halfway to her hairline.

Amy suppressed a groan. She hadn't intended to be quite so frank. Unfortunately the woman she was talking with was extremely adept at getting people to say more than they intended to. Ferreting out secrets was Naomi Pritikin's job. She was an investigative reporter.

Amy wondered if there was any way she could derail this line of questioning. If her previous ''girl talk'' brunches with her friend were anything to go by, she seriously doubted it.

Naomi continued, full speed ahead. ''You told me about his sending you roses and taking you out to dinner at that restaurant you used to go to,'' she said accusingly. ''But this is the first time you've mentioned sex!''

''Now wait a second. You're the one who mentioned—''

''What happened?''

''Naomi—''

"Come on, Amy. What happened?"

"Nothing happened."

"Nothing? You tried to seduce your ex-husband. He rejected you. You call that nothing?" Naomi leaned forward.

"It didn't happen like that!" Amy protested indignantly.

"No?" The brunette smiled sweetly, then relaxed back into her chair. "Then how did it happen?"

Amy sighed, shaking her head resignedly. She knew it was pointless to continue trying to evade Naomi's questions. "Doug walked me to my hotel room when we got back after dinner," she said. "We stood in the hallway and talked for a few minutes. Then . . . he kissed me."

"And you kissed him back." It was an assertion, not an inquiry.

"And I kissed him back." Amy shifted in her seat, feeling her pulse flutter at the memory.

"And then?" Naomi made a prompting gesture with one hand.

"And then, nothing. Doug . . . stopped."

Naomi frowned. "Because you were in the middle of a hotel hallway?"

Amy fiddled with her napkin. "So he said."

"Did you invite him in?"

"Not . . . exactly."

"But you did want him to—"

"More Bloody Marys, ladies?" a male voice interrupted.

"What?" Amy asked blankly. She turned slightly and looked up into the face of the tall, tanned and none too bright young waiter who had introduced himself as Cameron about ninety minutes before.

"More Bloody Marys?" he repeated.

"None for me," Naomi responded crisply. She pointed an elegantly manicured finger across the linen-draped table. "Two for her."

Cameron appeared to calculate. "You mean...a double?"

Amy spared Naomi a quick, sharp look, then returned her attention to the waiter. "No, thank you," she told him.

"But—" His forehead wrinkled like linen on a hot summer day.

"No," she repeated firmly. "Really. Nothing."

Cameron blinked several times, then his brow smoothed. "Oh." He glanced questioningly at Naomi. "You were, like, making a joke, right?"

"Right," she said.

He transferred his gaze to Amy. "And, like, you *really* don't want anything, right?"

"Right," Amy confirmed.

Cameron looked tremendously relieved. He flashed a set of blindingly white teeth. "Okay. That's cool," he declared amiably, then sauntered away.

"Are you trying to get me drunk?" Amy asked her friend once he'd ambled out of earshot.

Naomi lifted her napkin and dabbed at her lips. "Since you haven't been making all that much sense sober, I thought it might be worth a shot," she responded candidly. "Now, getting back to—"

"Naomi, I really don't want to talk about that."

Naomi frowned and drummed her fingers against the table. Then to Amy's surprise, she gave a small shrug. "All right," she agreed.

There was a brief pause. Amy fished a strawberry from the bowl of fresh fruit salad she'd ordered and nibbled on it. Naomi applied herself to her own food.

"I suppose I have sounded a bit confused today," Amy conceded eventually, referring back to her friend's previous comment.

Naomi made a dismissive gesture. "No problem. You *always* sound confused when you talk about your ex."

Amy's heart gave an odd little lurch. "Sorry."

"Don't apologize. You've listened to my incoherent ravings about the opposite sex plenty of times. Besides, you're a very intriguing case."

"Intriguing?"

"Umm-hmm." Naomi tapped the tines of her fork against her front teeth for a moment, then elaborated. "I've never met Doug, of course. But given all the things you've said—and haven't said—I think I know exactly why the two of you got together. What I *don't* have a clue about is why you broke up." She pulled a wryly cynical expression and put down the fork. "It's usually the other way around."

Amy traced a circle on the tablecloth with the tip of one finger. "Our divorce papers say irreconcilable differences."

Naomi rolled her eyes. "Which means anything from he drove you nuts by forgetting to put the cap back on the toothpaste to you found him in bed with your best friend and her pet sheep."

Amy had to smile.

The brunette steepled her fingers together. "Did you two ever fight?"

"Fight?"

"Yes, fight. You know. Screaming. Yelling. Throwing things. Did you and Doug ever behave like a normal married couple?"

"Well . . ."

"You didn't, did you?" Naomi sounded disapproving.

"We sometimes had . . . arguments," Amy said slowly.

"But never anything serious."

Amy knew what her friend was driving at. She sighed. "No. Never anything serious," she admitted. "There's nothing I can point to and say: 'This is where it started to go wrong.' I wish there were. I mean, understanding the mistakes you've made doesn't change the fact that you've made them. But it at least gives you a shot at trying to fix them."

"You think you've made mistakes?" There was a hint of challenge in the query.

"Isn't it obvious?"

"Just you? You're taking sole responsibility for screwing everything up?"

Amy grimaced. "It's not—oh, I don't know, Naomi! I've gone over it and over it in my mind, trying to figure out what happened between Doug and me."

"And?"

"And I keep remembering how *busy* we were. I'm not saying it wasn't exciting. It was. Doug and I knew what we wanted and we were working to get it. We were doing so well together, too. Only...only we *weren't* together—if you know what I mean."

Naomi seemed to mull this over. "Did you come to L.A. because you thought your marriage was falling apart?" she asked at last.

Amy felt a jolt of surprise. "No," she denied quickly. "I never thought—no! I came because the job I was offered was such an incredible opportunity. Doug was so proud of me. And my father! God, for the first time in my life, I actually—" She stopped abruptly.

Naomi pounced. "You actually what?" she demanded.

"Nothing," Amy answered flatly. "It doesn't really matter."

"Amy..."

Amy shook her head stubbornly. She was well aware that her friend could be as tenacious as a starving terrier with a juicy bone when it came to hanging on to topics that captured her interest. Normally she was amused by this particular facet of Naomi's personality. But not now. She had no intention of letting anyone chew over the subject of her relationship with her father.

There were a few tense seconds of silence, then Naomi heaved a sigh and eased back in her seat. "All right, all right," she said. "I can take a hint." She clicked her tongue and tilted her head. "Okay. So Doug encouraged you to take the job in L.A., right?"

"Right." The response was wary.

"Do you think *he* thought things were falling apart between the two of you?"

Amy's denial was even more vehement than her previous one. "Things weren't falling apart, Naomi," she insisted. "Not in the way you mean. And as for Doug encouraging me to take the job, well, neither one of us was crazy about the idea of a bi-coastal marriage. But we talked it out and we decided we could manage it. After all, we'd managed so much else."

"Doug never suggested you turn down the offer?"

"Of course not! He wouldn't do anything like that. He knew how much it meant to me."

"More than he did?"

Amy felt the blood drain out of her face. For a moment, she was afraid she might be physically ill. "Naomi, no. Oh, no."

"What about you? Did you ever bring up the possibility of your saying no and staying in New York?"

Amy was still too appalled by the implications of the previous question to be anything but utterly honest in her response. "I . . . I couldn't."

"Why not?"

"I just couldn't! Don't you see?"

Amy thought back, desperately trying to summon up reasoned, rational explanations for what she'd done. What she evoked instead was a frightening recollection of being overwhelmed by events . . . of being swept along by forces she'd help create but could no longer control. She felt her chest tighten and her heart begin to pound. Her vision wavered.

"Amy?" There was real alarm in Naomi's voice.

Amy drew a shuddery breath, struggling to fight free of the panic that threatened to engulf her. She focused on her friend's face.

"Are you all right?" Naomi asked.

Amy nearly laughed at the absurdity of the question. She was thankful she was able to choke back the sound. She knew it would have been unpleasant to listen to.

"No," she answered after a moment or two. "No, I'm not all right. I don't think I've been all right for a long time."

She chewed her lower lip, her mind slipping backward again. "We tried, you know," she said slowly, painfully. "We really tried to make it work after I took the job in Los Angeles. Doug would come out here one weekend. I'd go back there the next. We'd talk on the phone at least once a day. But it was so hard. I was tired. He was tired. There was never enough time." She shook her head. "At the end of nine months we just . . . oh, I don't know."

"At the end of nine months you and Doug realized the only things holding your marriage together were long-distance phone bills and frequent-flyer points?" Naomi suggested gently.

Amy wished some of her memories weren't quite so vivid. "That's how it seemed," she admitted.

"Which one of you suggested making the separation official?"

Amy massaged her left temple. "I—it doesn't really matter. We both knew. We both agreed."

"So you proceeded to get one of the most civilized divorces in history."

Amy couldn't quite get a fix on her friend's tone. "Doug and I were still—*are* still—friends," she said defensively.

"Uh-huh. And now your 'friend' has asked you to go away with him."

"I am *not* 'going away' with Doug, Naomi!" Amy objected. "I explained to you before."

"For heaven's sake, let's not start quibbling over the semantics of the arrangement again!" Naomi cut in. "You and your ex-husband are going to be in the same place at the same time and you're not going to be avoiding each other." She paused, her expression softening. "What do you want, Amy?"

Amy slumped in her seat. "Good question."

"So give me a good answer."

"I don't know."

"I think you do."

"No, I don't, Naomi." She shook her head. "Not any-more."

"You want to be with Doug again."

Amy averted her eyes. "We can't turn back the clock," she said, echoing the words she'd said three nights before in Rossellini's.

"Would you want to if you could?"

"I..." Amy's voice failed her for a few moments. "Only if I could figure out what I did wrong and put it right."

During the silence that followed, Amy asked herself if there was any possibility Doug felt the same way.

Five

———

Two weeks and one day later, Amy stepped gingerly out of a two-engine plane and onto the tarmac of a small municipal airport in upstate New York. She experienced a momentary urge to kiss the wonderfully solid—if rather oil-stained—surface beneath her stylishly shod feet, but she squared her slim shoulders and resisted the impulse. Squinting tiredly against the brightness of the late-afternoon sun, she glanced around, trying to get her bearings.

For the third time in, oh, no more than ten seconds, Amy asked herself if she knew what she was doing. The answer to the question was still no.

The commuter flight from LaGuardia Airport had been the final leg of a journey that had begun roughly seventy-two hours before in Tokyo. It also had been bumpy enough to shake loose several of the fillings in her back molars. Yet the physical turbulence she had endured during the trip paled in comparison with the emotional turmoil she felt when her eyes suddenly focused on the lean, dark-haired man who was coming out of the cinder-block building marked "Terminal."

Doug.

Her lips shaped his name.

Amy didn't know what she was doing. But if she was honest with herself, she knew she could sum up why she was doing it in a single syllable.

Slowly she began walking forward. Her heart seemed to thud three or four times for each step she took. The carry-on bag she had slung over one shoulder bumped heavily against her hip, making her high-heeled gait less than steady. A warm puff of wind ruffled her neatly styled hair. She brushed several stray strands back from her face with the sweep of one palm, then patted the tight little chignon at her nape.

Doug moved toward her with the powerfully graceful strides of the distance runner he had been in high school and college. He was clad in a pair of well-worn athletic shoes, faded jeans, a torso-hugging T-shirt and an old blue windbreaker. It had been years since Amy had seen him dressed in such a casual fashion. She'd become so accustomed to visualizing him in his impeccably tailored business attire— his "executive armor" as he called it—that she'd forgotten exactly how much informality suited him.

They came to a halt about two feet apart. Although Doug's eyes were hidden by a pair of mirrored, wire-rimmed sunglasses, Amy could feel them move over her in intimate assessment. Unsettled by her awareness of his scrutiny, she cocked her chin and stared back challengingly.

Doug's mouth twitched. He'd expected Amy to be a little prickly about his presence. They'd had a prolonged telephone discussion about her travel arrangements earlier in the week. She'd repeatedly insisted that she was perfectly capable of getting where she had to go by herself. He'd readily agreed that she was perfectly capable of damned near anything once she set her mind to it, then had flatly informed her that he still intended to be at the airport when her plane arrived.

There had been nine passengers on Amy's flight. Doug knew this because he'd sweated through eight unfamiliar faces before his ex-wife had finally appeared in the door of the small aircraft. He hadn't let himself acknowledge until that moment how unsure he'd been about whether she'd actually show up.

Even at a distance, Doug had sensed Amy's weariness and uncertainty. She'd looked as limp as a discarded tissue as she'd descended the metal exit steps. Then suddenly she'd drawn herself up, overcoming the exhaustion she was obviously feeling by sheer force of will. Doug had experienced a spurt of anxiety-tinged admiration as he'd watched the transformation.

Amy broke the silence between them the way a rock breaks glass.

"You didn't have to come," she declared without preamble. "I told you I could manage on my own." It seemed very important to her that she assert her independence—and her competence—right then and there.

Doug realized that his expectations about his ex-wife's mood had erred on the side of optimism. She was more than a little prickly. In fact, she was giving an excellent impression of a porcupine on full quill alert.

"It's nice to see you again, too, Amy," he answered mildly.

"Seriously, Doug."

"Oh, yes," he assured her immediately.

Doug watched the fine, fair skin above the bridge of Amy's nose pleat as her brows came together. The fact that she couldn't disguise her confusion over his apparent non sequitur told him how truly tired she was. Being confused meant being in less than perfect control, and he knew that was a situation his ex-wife had trouble tolerating. He also knew that she tried her damnedest to hide her moments of vulnerability.

"What?" she asked, her normally smooth voice slightly frayed.

"It's nice to see you again," he repeated calmly, shoving his sunglasses on top of his head. He paused a beat. "Seriously."

Amy stiffened and her eyes flashed a green that had nothing to do with the word *go*. For an instant, Doug thought she was genuinely going to lose her temper. He started to reach out toward her. Then something—perhaps it was the realization that he was being as deliberately provocative in his way as she was being in hers—caused her entire manner to change. After a few seconds, most of the tension melted out of her body. She shook her head, the beginnings of a very rueful smile tugging at the corners of her lips.

"You're going to be pleasant to me no matter what I do, right?" she asked with a trace of asperity.

Relief flooded through Doug. He spread his hands, palms upward. "I don't want to fight, Amy," he answered, watching her carefully.

She sustained his steady gaze for several moments, then dropped her eyes, fingering the wide leather strap of her over-the-shoulder bag. She heaved a long sigh. "Neither do I," she confessed, staring at the toes of her navy-and-white spectator pumps.

She was telling the truth. Despite the crabbiness of her opening remark, she didn't want to fight. Not now. Not with him. Exactly what she *did* want to do was...well, she wasn't ready to deal with that—yet.

In fact, Amy acknowledged unhappily, she wasn't ready to deal with much of anything at this point. Which undoubtedly was why she'd bristled at Doug. For all her protestations of being able to manage on her own, she realized that she was putting on an act. She also realized that her ex-husband was perceptive enough to recognize this. So rather than give him an opportunity to see that she felt as though she was hanging on to the end of her tether by her finger-nails, she'd gone on the offensive.

But he, for better or worse, had understood her intentions and refused to rise to her baiting.

"Amy?"

Slowly she looked up into Doug's attractive, intelligent face. She could read concern there. She could read questions, as well. And there was something else, too. Something more sensed than seen. Something that both soothed and stirred.

It was this "something else" that Amy responded to when she finally spoke.

She shifted her heavy shoulder bag. "Can we start this conversation over?" she asked.

The question contained an apology and an olive branch. Doug accepted both without hesitation. "Do you want to get back on the plane and come off again?" he suggested lightly.

Amy gave a brief laugh. "I was hoping we could pick things up right before the point where I should have said hello."

His lips curved upward, making the lines etched on either side of his mouth deepen. "Okay," he agreed, nodding. "Consider yourself picked up."

There was a short pause. Amy knew the next move was up to her. She put her memory on rewind. All right. All right. She'd just gotten off the plane. She'd spotted Doug, and she'd walked toward him. Now they were face-to-face, and he was waiting for her to speak.

Fresh air, fun and friendship, he'd promised her.

Sounds like old times, she'd observed.

Something like that, he'd responded.

Amy smoothed the skirt of her navy knit dress and cleared her throat.

"Hello, Doug," she said.

"Hello, Amy," he answered.

"It's nice to see you again." She moistened her lips with the tip of her tongue. "Umm...seriously."

Doug's right brow arched and she saw a spark of humor light the depths of his eyes. "It's nice to see you again, too," he replied.

Impulsively, Amy moved a half step forward. Going up on her toes, she brushed her mouth lightly against Doug's left cheek. His skin was smooth, telling her he'd probably shaved a short time before. His scent was clean and male, indicating he'd showered recently, as well.

"Thank you for coming to meet me," she murmured.

Her quick kiss caught Doug by surprise. So did her soft words. He didn't try to mask his reaction to either. "Even though you could have managed on your own?" he asked, his voice half rough, half velvet.

Amy's features tightened for a split second, then relaxed. "Especially since I could have managed on my own," she agreed.

"Exactly what have you got in this thing?" Doug demanded about ten minutes later, as he and Amy made their way across the airport parking lot. He had a white-knuckled grip on Amy's leather suitcase. "Lead bricks?"

"I warned you it was heavy," Amy reminded him, surreptitiously adjusting her carryon bag. She strongly suspected that the outline of the strap was now permanently embossed in the flesh of her right shoulder.

"So you did," he conceded. "Okay. Forget the lead bricks. Let me guess. Files from work, right?"

Amy shot him a quick, sideward glance, not quite sure whether the irritation she thought she heard in his voice was real. "I suppose you're going to tell me you came up here empty-handed?" she countered.

Doug grunted as the suitcase slammed into the side of his calf. "Actually, I *could* tell you that," he stated.

"Oh, really?"

"Really. I could tell you that—" he came to a halt and turned to face her "—but I'd be lying. The truth is, I brought a ton of paperwork with me, too." He put her suitcase down with a thump, then jerked his thumb to the right. "This is it."

As she opened her mouth to respond to his blunt admission about paperwork, Amy glanced in the direction he was indicating. What she saw momentarily deprived her of speech.

The "it" Doug had referred to was a convertible. A fire-engine-red convertible. A fire-engine-red convertible which, even to Amy's automotively untutored eyes, didn't look as though it had rolled off a Detroit assembly line anytime during the past two decades.

"What—what is that?" she asked faintly. The bag she had been carrying slipped off her shoulder and landed heavily on the asphalt.

Doug grinned, stroking the car's glossy scarlet surface. "A classic. I borrowed it from Sandy."

"Sandy? Your nephew Sandy?" Alexander "Sandy" Browne was Doug's oldest brother's oldest son. The last time Amy had seen him, he'd been a gawky young adolescent whose voice still wavered between registers in times of stress, just the way Doug's had at the same age. Surely Sandy couldn't be old enough to own a car.

"Sandy turned eighteen last month," Doug said, divining the direction of her thoughts with unnerving accuracy. "He bought the car from some junk dealer when he got his learner's permit. He's spent most of the last two years restoring it."

"He's eighteen...already?" Amy chewed her lip for a moment. "That's hard to believe."

"No kidding," Doug responded with a grimace. "I'm having a few problems dealing with the idea that the kid whose diapers I used to change is now an inch or two taller than I am." He shook his head. "Well, you know what they say: time flies when you're having fun."

For a moment, Amy thought Doug might mean this as some kind of criticism of her. Then she saw the expression in his eyes. If there was any reproach in his words, he clearly was directing it at himself.

"Yes, so they say," she echoed softly.

"They" were right—to a point, Amy reflected. Time *did* fly. But in her case at least, it seemed to be whizzing by at record speed whether she was having fun or not.

It had been years since Amy had ridden in a convertible with the top down. She'd forgotten how...seductive it could be.

The trip from the airport to her father's house was a long and circuitous one. It began unpromisingly. Doug kept his eyes fixed on the road ahead. Amy gazed out at the passing scenery, feeling a sense of constraint that had nothing to do with her snugly buckled seat belt. Neither she nor Doug said a word.

Gradually, however, the warmth of the sun and the soft rush of the wind began to exercise their special brand of magic. The press of weighty concerns eased. Knots of anxiety loosened.

After about ten minutes, Amy slipped off her shoes. She stretched her legs. The hem of her dress crept up. She automatically smoothed it back into place. Wiggling her toes, she luxuriated in the plush feel of the car's black carpeting and sighed approvingly.

A few minutes later, Amy reached up and plucked the pins out of her chignon, freeing her hair. She shook her head, sending coppery-brown strands fluttering over her face. She brushed them back with a careless scoop of her hands.

Amy sighed deeply and stretched again, shifting against the white vinyl upholstery of the seat. The hem of her dress slid up two...three...four inches. She didn't tug it back down this time. Instead, she crossed her slim legs, right over left, well above the knee. After a few seconds, she turned her head toward Doug.

"Do you want some music?" he asked unexpectedly. Although he still appeared to be concentrating on the ribbon of road unwinding in front of him, there was a quirk in the firm line of his lips that hinted he wasn't oblivious to what had been going on to his right. It seemed to Amy that his manner was much more relaxed than it had been at the start of the drive, too.

"Music?" She dug her toes into the thick carpeting. "Mmm—yes. Please."

"Check the glove compartment. There's supposed to be a bunch of tapes in there. Sandy said he had something we'd probably like."

Amy leaned forward. "'We?'"

"The only reason he let me borrow his pride and joy is because I told him I was meeting you."

"Oh." Amy popped the glove compartment open. More than a dozen plastic cassette cases spilled out. She culled through the assortment quickly. The song titles and recording artists listed on the first ten tapes were only vaguely familiar to her. The eleventh tape was a very different story. She gave a rueful laugh.

"What?" Doug asked.

"Golden Oldies," she informed him succinctly.

It was approaching dusk when they reached their destination.

"I hope the Gardiners were able to take care of everything," Amy murmured as she unlocked the front door of her childhood home. Bill and Nancy Gardiner were the local couple who looked after the house while her father was in Florida. After clearing her vacation plans with him two weeks before, she'd called the Gardiners and asked them to open the place.

"Don't worry," Doug said, pulling off his sunglasses and depositing them in the pocket of his windbreaker. "The utilities are back on and the phone's been reconnected. The refrigerator's even stocked up. I checked."

Amy batted a loose lock of hair off her face and gave him a startled look. "What?"

He smiled. "You told me you were going to ask the Gardiners to get things ready when we talked on the phone earlier this week, remember? I swung by this morning to make sure everything was squared away."

Amy pushed the door open. "But—"

"I used the key in the garage to let myself in," he said, correctly anticipating her question.

"Oh. Well, thank you."

"No problem."

It took a few moments to move her bags inside. Once that was done, Amy flicked on the hall light switch. She took a few seconds to reorient herself. The house was very still and the air seemed slightly stale. Except for the fact that the once solid green walls of the foyer were now covered with a buff-and-blue striped paper, everything was exactly as she remembered it.

Out of the corner of her eye, she saw Doug heft her suitcase. "Oh," she said quickly. "You don't have to."

He regarded her with a crooked grin. "I know I don't have to, Amy," he responded. "I want to."

She glanced toward the end of the foyer. "You *want* to lug lead bricks up a flight of stairs?"

Doug chuckled, running his free hand back through his hair. The movement pulled the stretchy fabric of his T-shirt taut against his leanly muscled chest. "Not really," he admitted candidly. "But I figure it's the only way I'm going to get to see your bedroom."

Amy blinked. "What?"

"Your bedroom. I've never seen it."

"Of course you've seen it."

He shook his head. "Nope."

"Doug, we've known each other since fourth grade."

"Think, Amy," he cut in. "Hilliard house rules. Your bedroom was always strictly off-limits to me. Even when we came to move your stuff after we were married, your father had everything boxed up and waiting in the foyer."

Amy frowned. It was true that her father had a very rigid sense of propriety. He'd always been strict with her. But still there must have been at least *one* occasion when Doug . . .

"Trust me," Doug said flatly. "If I'd actually seen your bedroom, I wouldn't have had to spend so much time fantasizing about it."

"You . . . fantasized about my bedroom?" Amy suspected he was teasing her, but she wasn't certain.

"Among other things." His voice was dry, his blue eyes very direct.

There was a momentary pause.

"Please," he said.

Amy felt slightly foolish. "You might be disappointed."

Doug grinned roguishly. "I'll take the risk."

"Wait a second!"

"Amy—"

"No. No. Just hold on, Doug."

They were now standing in front of the white wooden door that led to Amy's bedroom. Something about this situation had been nibbling annoyingly at the edge of her thoughts all the way up the stairs, and she'd suddenly realized what it was.

"You said you came over to check things out this morning," she reminded her ex-husband with a tinge of accusation. "Why didn't you look at my bedroom then?"

Doug set down Amy's suitcase and regarded her silently. The expression on his face triggered an odd sensation in the vicinity of her heart.

"I thought about it," he admitted finally. "But I couldn't. I know how you are about your privacy, Amy. Besides, I would have felt like a Peeping Tom."

"I see." His scruples didn't surprise her. Doug had always had a strong sense of honor. But they did touch her in a strange way. "You wouldn't feel like a Peeping Tom if I showed you around, hmm?" She rolled her eyes, realizing she'd just handed him a wonderful straight line.

He gave her a grin that said he knew a straight line when he heard it, but was going to be noble enough to resist making a wisecrack at her expense. "Nah," he answered. "I'd feel like a tourist."

"Maybe I should charge you admission," she retorted.

"Hey, I'll cough up a quarter if I think the room's worth it."

"A quarter?"

"Maybe more. Just let me in, okay?"

"Okay. If you insist."

And with that Amy opened the door to her bedroom and ushered her ex-husband inside. She couldn't help speculating about what he was expecting to see.

The room that had been hers for so many years was large and airy. It was done up in creamy white and multiple shades of blue. Her father had allowed her to redecorate as a sixteenth-birthday present.

It was a feminine room—there were eyelet lace-trimmed pillows on the twin beds, a faint hint of floral potpourri in the air—but it wasn't fussy. Amy's taste had always tended toward simplicity. She'd never been a collector or sentimental saver. She'd also been taught the importance of neatness and organization from an early age.

Crossing to the twin bed to the right of the door, Amy sat down on the edge of it. She looked at Doug, who had moved to the middle of the room. She watched as he stood there, slowly surveying his surroundings.

It was impossible to gauge his reaction, and this made her strangely nervous. She was also acutely conscious of the fact that the setting seemed to underscore his bred-in-the-bone masculinity. This awareness made her heart beat a little faster.

A minute or so passed.

"Well?" she finally asked, fluffing her wind-tangled hair with her fingers.

Pivoting on one heel, Doug turned toward her. He gave her an up-down-up assessment, as though trying to reconcile the woman she was now with the girl she had been when she'd lived in this room.

"It's very..." He paused, his sensually shaped mouth curling up at the corners. "Very virginal."

Amy felt her face warm, but she met his eyes steadily. "I..." She cleared her throat. "I was...very virginal for most of the years I lived here," she reminded him.

"Mmm." Doug seemed to concede the point. He glanced around another time, then brought his eyes back to hers. "Actually..." Another pause. Another movement of his mouth. Amy could tell he was preparing to say something outrageous. "It kind of makes me think of those blue-flowered panties you had in seventh grade."

The temperature of Amy's cheeks shot up. So did her pulse rate. "Bl-blue! Why you—" she sputtered, getting to her feet. "You *never* saw my underwear in seventh grade, Douglas Maxwell Browne!" She was not about to discuss in which grade he *had* seen her underwear.

"You mean you don't recall that beautiful spring day you and Trisha Powell were sitting on the top row of the bleachers at school and you suddenly realized Ken Dawkins, Jimmy Bergstrom and I were standing underneath you?"

A vivid image surfaced out of the pool of Amy's memories. "You were looking up my dress!" she gasped.

Doug hooked his thumbs into the belt loops of his jeans and nodded, unabashed.

"Ken and Jimmy, too?"

"Actually Jimmy was more interested in looking up Trisha's dress," he informed her offhandedly. "And Ken had lost his glasses, so he couldn't see much. Which is just as well. I probably would have had to pound him if he'd been able to."

She choked. "You—*what*?"

"I probably would have had to pound him," Doug repeated as though it were the most reasonable thing in the world to say. "Even back in seventh grade I felt a certain...ahem...proprietary interest in your panties."

Amy stared at him silently. While she had about as much insight into the workings of the adolescent male mind as she had into the workings of the adult one—which was little or none—she sensed Doug was telling the absolute truth. Slowly she reseated herself on the bed.

"You're not offended, are you?" Doug asked.

"Offended?" she echoed. "Why? Because you've just admitted to being an underwear freak?"

A devilish gleam blazed up in the depths of his blue eyes. "Surely you had some clue before this."

Amy shifted, suddenly uneasy. The tone of this discussion was becoming a little too provocative for her. "Doug—"

"I meant it as a compliment, you know," he interrupted, the gleam in his eyes cooling.

She blinked, trying to make sense of what seemed to be a kangaroo jump from one topic to another. "What?" she asked.

He made a gesture with his right hand. "What I said about your room. I meant it as a compliment."

"Oh." Amy let a few seconds go by. "This is a very strange conversation," she complained.

Doug studied her for a moment. "This is a very strange situation," he countered quietly.

Amy's heart did a sudden flip-flop at his shift of tone. She opened her mouth to point out that this "situation" was rooted in a suggestion *he* had made. But before she had a chance to speak, Doug changed gears once again.

"You know, there's another thing your bedroom makes me think of," he observed reflectively. "And that's those sleep-overs you used to have with Trisha and Katie Lynde."

Amy experienced an unexpected pang of nostalgia. "Pajama parties," she amended with a wistful laugh, then shot her ex-husband a sharp glance. "If you tell me you and Ken and Jimmy figured out some way to spy on us, you're in serious trouble," she warned.

"We *did* give some thought to it," Doug conceded with a chuckle. "But Jimmy was scared of heights, I was scared of your father, and Ken was just plain chicken." He paused, eyeing Amy speculatively. "Exactly what went on at those sleep-overs, anyway? I mean ... what did you talk about?"

Amy lifted her chin. "I'll never tell."

"Come on."

She shook her head.

"Please?"

"Conversations at pajama parties are classified."

"Just give me a hint."

"No."

"Amy—"

"You've never told me what you and your friends used to talk about while you were off on those stupid camping trips of yours."

"That's different!"

"Oh, really?"

"For crying out." Doug looked aggrieved. "What do you think we used to talk about? It was *guy* stuff, Amy."

"Fine. What Trisha, Katie and I used to talk about was *girl* stuff."

Doug folded his arms across his chest. "Tit for tat?"

"Quid pro quo."

"You tell me. I tell you."

"Only if you go first."

Doug rolled his eyes. "You drive a hard bargain, lady."

Amy smiled sweetly. "I'm a MBA, remember?"

"You really want to know?"

"Definitely."

"Okay. Okay," he acquiesced. "We used to talk about sports. A lot about sports. School ... once in a while. And of course sex." He grinned wickedly. "I seem to remember we spent some time discussing the size of Daphne Trott's...!" He cupped the air in front of his chest.

"Doug!" Amy snatched one of the eyelet throw pillows off the bed she was sitting on and fired it at his head.

"Hey!" Doug fielded the down-stuffed missile deftly. "You asked me. I told you." He waited a beat, kneading the pillow between his hands. "Your turn."

Amy frowned.

"Come on, Amy," he prompted. "We had an oral contract."

Amy sat up straight, primly folding her hands in her lap. "All right," she sighed. "We talked a lot about makeup and clothes. And school. And...boys."

"Uh-huh."

"We...may even have discussed Daphne Trott," she admitted. She paused for a moment or two, then added with uncharacteristic cattiness, "That wasn't all her. At least, not in junior high."

"Yeah, I know," came the smug reply.

"You know?"

Doug held the pillow up in front of him as though fending off Amy's indignant question. "Strictly hearsay," he declared quickly.

Amy regarded him narrowly for a good five seconds, then sniffed and looked away. She was play-acting, of course. Going along with a gag from the good old days when everything had been so simple.

And yet, deep within her, she was conscious of the gnaw of an emotion that was as unwarranted as it was unpleasant. She had no reason...no *right*...to feel jealous. But she did. And not just about Daphne Trott's bust, either.

Doug closed the distance between them in three lithe strides. After a fractional hesitation, he sat down next to his ex-wife. "Hey," he said, nudging her gently. "I swear, I don't know what Daphne Trott did—or didn't—have in her bra. And frankly I never really cared to find out."

His physical proximity was disturbing. Amy was acutely aware of the warmth of his body, the clean scent of his skin. She swallowed, trying to dislodge the lump that had coalesced in her throat.

"Amy?" Doug's voice was soft and shorn of all bantering inflections.

Slowly Amy turned her face back toward his. "For somebody who never really cared, you certainly spent a lot of time looking," she observed, striving for a teasing tone and almost achieving it.

Doug studied her for several long moments. His forehead was slightly furrowed, his lips were thinned into a straight line. His eyes were very clear and very keen and Amy could sense the clear, keen brain behind them assessing...asking questions. Maybe even arriving at answers.

The possibility sent a tiny frisson of panic dancing up her spine.

Suddenly, surprisingly, Doug's mouth quirked. "Well," he responded dryly, "it was kind of hard to miss. Especially since my nose was about level with Daphne's—ah—chest back in junior high."

Amy managed a weak laugh. "I see your point," she conceded.

"You usually do."

There was a silence then. An expectant silence, tinged with equal parts of anticipation and anxiety.

Amy toyed with her hair, straining the wind-blown strands through the fingers of one hand. She shifted her weight. The restless movement brought her thigh into brief, brushing contact with Doug's. She felt him stiffen, heard him inhale sharply.

Gray-green eyes met blue ones. Amy bit her lower lip as muscles deep within her clenched tight as a fist, then released in a liquid throb. She was conscious of a sudden aching in her breasts...of the almost painful tightening of their tips. Her heart was pounding.

"Amy." Doug brought both hands up and stroked her hair back behind her ears. Then he cradled her face between his palms. The tender drift of his thumbs along the line of her jaw made her tremble.

She was never certain where she found the strength—if strength was the right word—to do what she did next.

What she did was to shake her head "no"...and mean it.

Six

"Now, that wasn't so bad," Doug observed shortly before noon the following day. "Was it, Amy?"

"I wasn't expecting it to be *bad*, Doug," she countered.

"But you weren't looking forward to it, either."

"True."

"You were afraid it would be awkward."

"Well, put yourself in my place. Wouldn't you feel the same way?"

"I told you, our divorce isn't a problem."

"You told me, but I don't believe you. Anyway, it's more than that."

"What else?"

"You know."

"No, I—oh, God!" He started to laugh. "Don't tell me you're still hung up about that after all these years!"

"It's not funny, Doug."

"Yes, it is. For the zillion-and-first time: My mother thinks you're a 'nice' girl." He paused a beat, then added provocatively: "*Despite* the fact that she knows you used your feminine wiles to seduce me, her innocent, blue-eyed baby boy."

"Why, you—" Amy was sorely tempted to give her ex-husband a good, swift kick. She resisted the retaliatory urge because Doug was driving and she didn't want to cause a traffic accident.

Doug flicked on the turn signal. He'd had to return the fire-engine-red convertible to his nephew Sandy's custody the previous evening, so he was back behind the wheel of his own six-month-old BMW, which he'd driven up from Manhattan.

"I can't believe you're still upset about that time Mom called my dorm room at college and you answered the phone," he said, shaking his head and taking a smooth right.

"It was very embarrassing!" Amy defended herself. "It was seven o'clock on a Saturday morning. Even though I was half asleep, she recognized my voice right away. I knew what she had to think."

"Did you seriously believe she'd buy your line about being there because we were studying for finals?"

The memory of one of the most mortifying episodes in Amy's life made her face heat. While she'd certainly never felt any shame about the fact that she and Doug had been lovers before they'd gotten married, she'd been less than sanguine about his mother's awareness of the situation.

She'd had more than a few problems coping with her father's discovery of the truth, too, but her father was now hundreds of miles away in Florida. She hadn't had to spend thirty minutes chitchatting with him as she'd just done with Beth Browne.

"Amy?" Doug prompted.

"Oh, all right. I admit it was a lame explanation."

"Lame? It was the first week in October!" Doug brought his car to a halt at a four-way intersection, then glanced at Amy. She was frowning and her cheeks were faintly flushed.

Reaching over, he stroked the back of his hand lightly against the side of her face. "Hey, it's okay, Amy. After all, my mother wasn't exactly oblivious to how things were between you and me—even before that phone call."

"Oh?" Amy shifted, brushing at her hair. Although the touch of his hand had been brief, it had made her body tingle clear down to her toes.

"Remember that big bag of laundry I lugged home at Christmas break freshman year?"

She nodded.

"Well, not everything in it was mine."

Amy groaned her comprehension.

"You got it," Doug confirmed dryly. "Of course my mother *could* have jumped to the conclusion that I'd developed a very kinky taste in clothes during my first semester at college. But given that two of the items that turned up had the initials A.H. embroidered on them..." The traffic light hanging in the middle of the intersection changed colors. Doug transferred his foot from the brake to the gas pedal.

"Did . . . did she say anything to you?"

Doug shook his head, his eyes back on the road. "A couple of days after Christmas my dad sat me down for this very serious man-to-man discussion. It was sort of a graduate-level version of the birds-and-bees lecture he gave me when I was about thirteen. To tell the truth, I couldn't figure out why the hell he was doing it until he handed me a brown paper bag with your freshly washed stuff in it." He chuckled ruefully. "I was so shocked, I couldn't speak. Which is probably just as well, all things considered. Lord only knows what I would have told him."

Amy had to laugh. "Something as bad as my story about studying for finals?"

"Worse," he assured her. "Much worse."

They traveled in silence for a minute or two.

"This was the first time I've seen your mother since we got divorced," Amy commented finally, looking down at her hands.

"I know."

"I guess I wasn't expecting her to be so nice," Amy confessed. The half hour she'd just spent with Beth Browne had been a surprisingly enjoyable one. While Doug's mother had seemed to be choosing her words with more care than Amy remembered her doing in the past, her overall manner had been friendly. She had sensed the older woman studying her covertly several times, but she supposed some show of curiosity was understandable.

"She doesn't blame you for the divorce, Amy," Doug said. "She really doesn't. Now she certainly wasn't happy when we decided to split up. Neither was my dad, for that matter. They both like you very much. But they also realize that things happen. That people change."

In all truth, Doug had endured quite a few anxious moments in connection with this morning's visit. His parents knew about his mild heart attack and the impact it had had on his life. They also knew that he had yet to tell Amy about his illness; about his decision to quit Allan, Chandler, Marchand and Lee and join his father's practice; or about his true reasons for suggesting she spend her vacation in their old hometown.

His mother had made it clear that she enthusiastically endorsed what her youngest son wanted to do—particularly if it meant a reconciliation with Amy. But she'd also plainly stated that she didn't approve of his tactics one single bit. Nonetheless, she'd agreed to keep quiet. Despite this pledge of discretion, Doug had been worried that she'd let something slip. Fortunately she hadn't.

Amy knit her fingers together, then unraveled them. Although Doug's words about his parents' attitudes toward her had been reassuring, they weren't enough to set her mind completely at ease. She sighed heavily.

"What?" Doug asked, taking a left turn.

"Nothing."

"That sigh didn't sound like nothing. Come on, Amy."

She hesitated for a few seconds, worrying her lower lip with her teeth and grappling with the real reason she'd felt so uncomfortable around Beth Browne. "Your parents must think it's...strange...for me to be up here," she said at last.

The adjective seemed to reverberate within the confines of the car, evoking memories of their encounter in her innocently pretty white-and-blue bedroom. Amy wasn't certain whether she'd chosen the word deliberately, or whether it had just slipped out.

"A little, maybe," Doug conceded carefully. "But they understand how things are between us."

Amy gave a tinder-dry laugh. She was glad to hear *somebody* did, especially given some of the events of the past twenty-four hours. "And how's that?" she asked.

Doug slanted a quick look at her. "We're still friends...aren't we?"

There was another pause. Amy shifted her position and picked a minuscule bit of lint off her khaki cotton slacks. She knew what needed to be said next. Like the toppling of a line of dominoes, there was a kind of inevitability to it. She opened her mouth.

"About what happened yesterday—"

"About what happened yesterday—"

Both she and Doug spoke in the same instant. They stopped simultaneously, too.

"Sorry, I didn't mean to—"

"Sorry, I didn't mean to—"

Again, they began and halted in unison.

"Stereo," Doug joked. "Ladies first."

"No...no," Amy refused quickly. "You go."

"You sure?"

She nodded. "Yes."

Doug took a few moments to collect his thoughts and consider his words. His lean fingers tightened on the steering wheel. "I shouldn't have come on to you the way I did," he said flatly. "It wasn't something I'd planned—despite the cracks about fantasies and blue-flowered underpants. I didn't go up to your bedroom intending to make a pass. It just . . . happened. Please believe me, Amy.''

"I believe you, Doug," she replied quietly, thinking back to a scene in a New York City hotel hallway.

"Thank you."

"You're welcome."

"I guess . . ." His tone was wryly reflective. "I guess that finally getting into the sanctum sanctorum after so many years went to my head."

It had been more than that, of course, Doug acknowledged silently. It had been the spice-sweet scent of her perfume, tantalizing his nostrils. The artless disarray of her copper-brown hair, tempting his fingers. And the teasing sparkle of her wide hazel eyes, triggering memories of the countless times in their relationship that laughter had turned to loving.

There had been only inches between them when he'd sat down next to Amy on the bed. She'd been so close. And she'd gotten closer still when she'd shifted, betraying her awareness of his nearness.

She'd seemed so . . . so damned vulnerable, too. And that as much as anything else had made him reach out and touch her. He'd felt the need to comfort, as well as caress. You need me, he'd wanted to tell her. You need me as much as I need you.

The sound of Amy's voice—questioning, slightly hesitant—brought Doug out of his reverie with a start. He stiffened, realizing he'd been so intent on reliving what had happened between them the day before that he'd almost forgotten he was driving. Fortunately the road they were on was relatively straight and virtually free of traffic.

"Doug?"

"Ah—sorry, Amy," he apologized quickly. He glanced to his right for a second, then brought his eyes front and center once more. "I was . . . thinking."

His obvious distraction surprised Amy. It wasn't like Doug to retreat into himself. At least, it *hadn't* been like him. She thought again of the changes she'd sensed in him nearly three weeks before in New York City.

"Are you all right?" she asked, studying his strong profile. She saw his jaw tense as though he was clenching his back teeth.

"Fine," Doug responded, conscious that his palms weren't completely dry. The usually comfortable fit of his chino pants suddenly seemed a bit too snug, as well. "Just fine."

"You're not...angry, are you?"

He looked to his right again. "At you?"

She nodded. "Because I said no."

"Of course not." Doug returned his gaze to the road. "Look, I'm not going to tell you I was happy you stopped things when you did. But it was the right thing to do. When I suggested you come up here, I promised you there were no strings. I meant it."

Yes, he had promised her that. And yes, at the time he'd made the pledge, he had probably believed he meant it. But deep in his gut, Doug knew he'd lied.

There were plenty of "strings" attached to his suggestion about how Amy might spend her vacation. Strings he intended to use to weave their lives back together. He just hoped those strings didn't end up tripping or choking him.

Amy said nothing for several seconds, trying to channel the turbulent surge of emotion welling up within her. She wasn't happy that she'd stopped things when she did the previous day, either. She'd *needed* Doug. She'd needed to be held and hugged and made to feel whole.

And yet the thought of depending so desperately on anyone, even Doug, had been frightening to her. The thought of revealing that dependence to anyone—*especially* Doug— had been even more terrifying. She'd earned his love by being strong and sure. She couldn't risk forfeiting whatever feelings he had left for her by showing herself to be weak and wanting.

"I . . . I'm not exactly certain what I'm doing here," she finally confessed with an awkward laugh.

"Give yourself some time, sweetheart," Doug replied. "You'll figure it out."

"Well?" Doug asked expectantly about forty minutes later. He and Amy were standing in the kitchen of his new home. He'd just finished giving her a tour of the place.

"I...um..." Amy paused, hearing a dull thump-thump-thump from above. She looked up, wondering whether she should start preparing to dodge falling chunks of plaster. Luckily everything looked reasonably secure—including the cobweb-covered light fixture directly over her head.

"I guess the roofer's back from his lunch break," Doug observed prosaically, putting his hands in the pockets of his trousers and watching Amy's face.

"It's too bad about the leak."

"Yeah. It ruined the wallpaper in the upstairs hall."

"You . . . like . . . that paper?" She couldn't imagine what could have prompted someone to select magenta, mauve and mint paisley wallpaper for the upstairs hall. Mere lack of good taste wasn't an adequate explanation.

"I've seen worse," Doug said, shrugging. "Now, come on. You've had the grand house-and-garden tour. What do you think?"

"Well..."

"Try to imagine it without the asbestos siding. That's all coming off."

"Oh, good." Amy nodded approvingly. The asbestos siding in question bore a vague resemblance to pinky-brown rhinoceros hide.

"So?" Doug prompted patiently.

"So..." She gestured. "It's not exactly what I expected."

"Which means?"

"Well, it's so big, for one thing." In point of fact, it was about six rooms and two porches bigger than she had envisioned. "You described it as a vacation place. And your mother called it a cottage."

" 'Cottage' in quotation marks. A Victorian 'cottage.' "

"That's another thing, Doug. *Victorian?* I thought you were a believer in the Bauhaus school of architecture. You know, less is more?"

"I'm learning to be flexible," he returned easily. Taking his hands out of his pockets, he crossed his arms over his chest and leaned back against the edge of one of the tiled counters.

"Flexible." Amy echoed, not at all certain what that meant.

She glanced around the kitchen again, taking in the finely detailed molding and the wainscoted cabinets. Everything was in dire need of repainting, she noted with a grimace. And one of the walls looked as though it had contracted the heartbreak of psoriasis. Still, there was *something*...

Her initial impression of the house had been negative. The unmitigated ugliness of the exterior asbestos siding had stunned her so badly that she couldn't speak, much less produce a convincing white lie about the eccentric charm of the place.

Things hadn't improved once Doug had ushered her inside. At least, not at first. Then slowly Amy had begun to notice hints of potential. She'd sensed the presence of possibilities. Suddenly she'd been aware that an odd tingle of excitement was running through her. The sensation reminded her of the feeling she got when she analyzed the balance sheet of a supposedly run-into-the-ground company and discovered that there was life in the old firm yet. Yes, there definitely was *something* about this house...

"You don't like it?" Doug asked.

Amy started. "I haven't said that," she snapped, brushing her hair back behind her ears.

He raised his brows. "Actually you haven't said much at all," he remarked.

"For heaven's sake, give me a chance!" More than a little nettled, Amy found herself wondering why Doug was so interested her opinion about his new vacation house. She was on the verge of demanding an explanation when her ex-husband forestalled her.

"You think it's falling to pieces, right?"

"I wouldn't go that far, Doug. But—"

"It's been neglected. And it's rundown."

"Well—"

"To tell the truth, I felt the same way the first time I looked at it."

Amy was taken aback by this blunt admission. "You—you did?"

Doug nodded. "Then I took another good, hard look. There's nothing fundamentally wrong with this place. The foundation's solid. It's structurally sound. Sure, it's got some peculiarities and sure, it needs a lot of work. But it's worth it, Amy. I know it's worth it. With the right amount of time and TLC..."

Doug wasn't looking at his surroundings when he spoke. He was looking directly at her, determination blazing in his brilliant blue eyes. That determination—and the potent conviction in his voice—make Amy go weak in the knees. Her breath jammed at the top of her throat. She swallowed hard and reached for the edge of a counter.

"With the right amount of time and TLC—what?" she questioned huskily.

She saw Doug blink. The fire in his gaze was banked down in an instant. His tone, when he responded, was light...almost teasing.

"With the right amount of time and TLC, just about anything can be salvaged," he told her. Then he smiled and asked, "Want to help?"

"Owww!" Amy yelped, dropping the claw hammer and nail punch she'd been wielding and cradled her throbbing left hand against her chest. She sat back on the heels of her sneakered feet, swearing under her breath.

Doug materialized in the doorway of the living room a moment later.

"What happened?" he asked sharply. He was dressed in old jeans and a faded blue work shirt. While he'd tucked the shirt in, he hadn't bothered to button it. The garment had gaped open to reveal an inverted triangle of dark hair that narrowed into a fine line of down before disappearing beneath the low-riding waistband of his denims.

"What do you think happened?" Amy retorted, glaring. "I bashed my damned thumb with the damned hammer while trying to punch some nail head below the surface of some board so this damned wooden floor will be ready for that damned sanding machine you rented!"

"Now, that's a damned shame," Doug replied straight-faced. He moved to where Amy was kneeling and hunkered down beside her. "Let me see," he instructed.

After a brief show of reluctance, Amy acquiesced and extended her left hand. Doug studied her injured thumb for a few seconds, then began to manipulate it very gently.

Amy bit the inside of her lip. Doug's deft ministrations had set off as many tingles of pleasure as twinges of pain. Both sensations danced along her nervous system, jangling awake feelings she'd have preferred remain dormant.

The past week had been one of the sweetest, yet strangest, of her life. She'd spent a significant part of it in her ex-husband's company, laboring side-by-side with him on his "new" house.

Of course, working on the house was exhausting in many ways. Amy certainly hadn't had any problems with insomnia during the past six nights! But the job was exhilarating, as well. While their restoration project was far from finished, she could already see tangible proof of her ex-husband's assertion about the positive effects of time and TLC.

As for her relationship with her ex-husband...well, Amy *still* wasn't sure what was going on. Despite their teamwork during the daylight hours, she and Doug spent their nights apart. She returned to her father's house to delve into the files she'd brought from Los Angeles. He remained behind to work on a mountainous stack of legal paperwork. Although they indulged in a certain amount of physical teasing and verbal flirtation when they were together, there'd been no repetition of their encounter in her girlhood bedroom.

Amy had no doubt that Doug wanted to make love with her. She could sense it in the glances he gave her when he thought she wasn't looking. She could feel it in the way his fingers lingered on hers when their hands brushed during the course of a shared task. Yet day after day her ex-husband would go so far...and no farther.

She also had no doubt that she wanted to make love with him. There were irrational moments, triggered by things as insignificant as the way his dark hair clung and curled at the back of his neck, when the desire she felt for Doug burned so hotly that she couldn't speak or move for fear of betraying it. Yet day after day she would go so far...and no farther.

Amy didn't know whether this setting of limits was Doug's doing or hers or a combination of both. A part of her resented what was—or wasn't—happening. Another part was enormously relieved by it.

Amy had never thought of herself as a go-with-the-flow kind of person. Yet that was what she'd been doing during the past week. She hadn't been drifting exactly. But she certainly hadn't been making much of an effort to challenge the tide of events, either.

She'd realized that her uncharacteristic passivity was an attempt to protect herself. The defenses she'd spent so many years building had been undermined by forces she couldn't figure out how to fight. Deep down, she was afraid that who she was—*what* she was—was in jeopardy because of it. So she was just letting the situation ride...

There were times when the urge to confide in Doug was very, very strong. But dear God, what could she say to him? How could she tell him that her job—her supposedly wonderful, fulfilling job—seemed to be as enervating as it was empty? How could she tell him that she kept looking at what she'd worked so hard to achieve and wondering whether it meant anything?

How could she tell him that she realized she'd taken a wrong turn in her life but that she didn't know when or where or why or how to get started back in the right direction?

"Amy?"

The sound of Doug's voice jerked Amy out of her troubled and troubling reverie.

"Wh-what?" she questioned, meeting his inquiring gaze for a moment, then turning her attention to her thumb. He still had possession of her left hand. She wondered distractedly how long she had been caught up in her reflections. "Did you—I didn't hear the question."

"I asked if this—" *this* was a careful wiggling of her knuckle "—hurts."

Amy winced. "No."

"Uh-huh," came the skeptical response. Doug clicked his tongue against the roof of his mouth, apparently considering his diagnosis.

"If you say anything about hacksaws or amputations, you'll regret it," Amy informed him.

"I don't think things are quite that bad," he answered with a smile. Then before Amy realized what he intended, he'd raised her hand to his lips and kissed the tip of her thumb.

"D-Doug." A sudden shortness of breath robbed her planned remonstration of force.

"I could suck it for you, too," he offered with a mock leer.

"Doug!" Without considering the consequences, Amy snatched her hand out of his and took a swat at him. Her abused thumb connected with a rock-hard bicep. "Yee-ouch!" she squawked.

While Amy's blow had no apparent effect on Doug, the fact that he started laughing in the wake of it caused him to lose his balance. He toppled over, landing awkwardly on his rear end. This only increased his mirth.

Despite the self-inflicted damage to her thumb and dignity, Amy began giggling. "St-stop th-that!" she demanded, fighting a losing battle for self-control. "This . . . this isn't f-funny!"

"Yes, it is."

"No, it's not!"

"Then why—" Doug paused long enough to draw a gasping breath. "Then why are you laughing?"

"B-because . . ." Her giggles were multiplying faster than a bunch of sex-crazed bunnies. "Because it m-makes me forget how m-much my thumb hurts!"

Amy had no idea how many minutes the two of them spent sprawled on the living-room floor, hooting and howling as though they'd been dosed with laughing gas. She didn't really care. The release felt absolutely marvelous.

Eventually their hilarity ran down. Amy struggled to a sitting position, her giggles giving way to a series of hic-cupy sighs. She wiped at her eyes. Doug sat up, too, his whoops of laughter moderating into an occasional chortle.

"What are you wearing under that sh-hic!—shirt!?" Amy asked. "Body armor?"

Doug's mouth twisted at the backhanded compliment to his muscle tone. "It's just me. Want to see?" He made a movement as though he was about to start disrobing.

"No!" Amy refused hastily.

He gave her a reproving look. "You don't have to yell. And you didn't have to haul off and hit me, either."

"Oh? What you said about my thumb was disgusting."

"Disgusting?" His brows went up. "I offered to suck your thumb to make it feel better. That's a pretty generous offer, considering I don't know where it's been."

"Doug!"

"Well, I don't," he insisted, then frowned. "By the way, what's that purple-green crud under your nails?"

Amy looked down at her hands and grimaced. "It's residue from the upstairs-hall wallpaper."

"We finished stripping that two days ago."

"No kidding. I think the stain may be permanent."

"Well, I owe you a manicure."

"You owe me a lot more than that, Doug." Amy massaged her thumb and surveyed her ex-husband for several seconds. Laughter had erased years from his features. His blue eyes were as clear as a perfect summer sky. "Do you happen to know a good lawyer? I'm thinking about filing a lawsuit."

Doug cocked his head. His dark hair was dusted with white flecks. It looked like dandruff, but Amy knew it was spackling.

"A lawyer?" he repeated. "What's wrong with me?"

"You're the one I'm thinking about filing the suit against."

"What did I do? Hey, offering to suck a woman's thumb isn't even a misdemeanor in this state."

"Forget my thumb. You got me up here under false pretenses."

Doug stiffened, then went very still. "I..." He plowed the fingers of one hand back through his hair, releasing a blizzard of tiny white flakes. "What makes you say that, Amy?"

Amy paused for a moment, trying to puzzle out his expression. There was something *odd* about it. Something anxious. It was almost as though Doug was afraid of how she was going to respond to his question? Was that it? Was it fear she was seeing? But why?

"Amy?"

She blinked once. Suddenly the expression was gone from his face. Completely vanished. As though it had never been there at all.

Maybe it hadn't been, Amy thought. Maybe she'd unconsciously projected her own turbulent emotions onto him.

"Amy?" Doug repeated.

She shook her head, trying to clear it. "When you suggested I come up here, you mentioned fresh air, fun and friendship. You didn't say anything about physical labor."

"Ah." The sound came out in a long, sighing exhalation. Doug smiled crookedly and leaned back, propping himself up with his hands. "That was in the fine print, sweetheart."

"Hey!" Doug exclaimed late in the afternoon of the following day. He and Amy were in the local hardware store picking up supplies and bickering over color schemes.

"Hey, what?" Amy pivoted and glanced at the paint chip he was holding out to her. It was a virulent shade of purple. "Oh, ugh, Doug! That's hideous!"

"Didn't you used to have a lipstick this color?" he inquired slyly.

"Of course not!" she denied vehemently, then darted another look at the paint sample in Doug's hand. She was suddenly assailed by an acute feeling of déjà vu.

Doug watched the dawn of recollection tint Amy's cheeks. "It's all coming back, right?"

"Ah—"

"It was one of those flavored kinds. It tasted like...mmm..." Doug ran his tongue over his lips. Amy groaned. "Like cheap artificial grape juice."

"Doug!"

"You started wearing it around the time you got your first pair of fishnet stockings."

Amy gave him a measuring look. "As an attorney, I'm sure you realize that reminding a woman of her high-school wardrobe is considered justification for homicide in a lot of places, don't you?'' she inquired sweetly.

"I thought those stockings were . . . cute."

"Oh, right," came the acerbic retort. "They were about as cute as that Nehru jacket you had."

Doug clasped his hands over his heart. "Cruel, Amy. Extremely cruel."

"As a matter of fact, I'm pretty sure there's a picture of you wearing that jacket in one of the albums back in my father's attic," she continued smugly. "There's probably one of you in your tie-dyed bell-bottoms, too. Remember? The ones you had when your hair was longer than mine?"

"You tell anybody about that and I'll sue for defamation of character," Doug threatened. "Better yet, I'll find a picture of you wearing white plastic go-go boots and send it to the *Wall Street Journal*!"

Amy realized she'd been beaten. She might as well acknowledge all her fashion sins. She turned back to the paint samples and homed in on a sickeningly sweet, spun-sugar pink. After plucking it out of the rack, she showed it to Doug.

"I had a lipstick in this color, too," she admitted.

Doug smiled. "I remember. It tasted like bubble gum."

There was a tiny pause. Then with great deliberation, Doug lifted his right hand and outlined Amy's mouth with the work-roughened pad of his thumb. Her lips were moist with a hint of tinted gloss. The cosmetic was slick and smooth. The mouth it enhanced was tender and starting to tremble.

Amy whispered his name. Her warm breath misted his hand in a butterfly-light caress.

"You know, it's funny," he mused aloud. "But the older I get, the more I appreciate the *natural* flavor of things."

For ten mornings in a row, Doug had gotten out of bed promising himself that this was going to be the day he told Amy the truth. The whole truth.

For nine nights in a row, he'd gotten into bed knowing that he'd broken his word.

I can't just burst out with it, he told himself, scrubbing at a particularly stubborn stain on the kitchen floor. Amy was a few feet away on a stepladder, painstakingly cleaning the wainscoted fronts of the cabinets. I can't. Not yet. I have to pick the right time. The right place.

Doug knew not telling Amy was wrong. And cowardly, to boot. But he was afraid. Afraid of what would happen if he continued to keep silent. Afraid of what would happen if he didn't.

Did Amy feel the turmoil in him? Doug wasn't sure. He'd felt her watching him, and caught glimpses of questions in her eyes when he'd turned in response to the almost tangible touch of her gaze. He'd sensed her intuition quivering, too, on the many occasions when he'd teetered on the brink of pouring everything out.

Still, Amy had refrained from pushing and probing the way she had pushed and probed during the first ten minutes of their meeting over drinks back in Manhattan. Lord, she'd done everything she could to discover the real reason he'd sent the blush-pink roses to her! As awkward as the verbal fencing had been, Doug knew he'd taken an almost erotic enjoyment from matching wits with her. Part of him had been deeply disappointed when she'd finally given up her deft inquisition.

Doug thought he understood why she'd disengaged. Amy had always been very shrewd about picking her battles and preserving her resources. He remembered teasing her once about always being successful at the things she chose to do. She'd gotten the strangest look on her face—half fierce, half frightened—and told him that she always succeeded because she never chose to do things at which she might fail.

Thriving on risks and challenges as he did, Doug had assumed at the time that Amy was making a joke. Eventually he had abandoned that assumption. Amy Anne Hilliard didn't take chances.

Perhaps that was the key reason he was holding back from telling her the truth. Doug knew he was eventually going to have to ask his ex-wife to make some tremendous choices—to take what might seem like a terrifying chance. Lord knew, had anyone suggested *before* his heart attack that he should do what he'd decided to do *after* it, he would have thought they were completely crazy!

It had taken a brush with death to open his eyes to what he'd been doing to himself and his life. Doug didn't want Amy to have to endure anything like that. He was hoping that "fresh air, fun and friendship" would make her see that the fast lane she was racing along was not the only road open to her. He was hoping that things would be so good between them, that the choices he prayed she would make wouldn't seem like such awful chances.

Amy wasn't happy. Doug sensed that with every fiber of his being. He wasn't arrogant enough to believe he was the sole cause of whatever was wrong with her. Nor was he arrogant enough to believe he could be the sole cure. But dammit, he knew he had been, was and always would be a vital part of her life—just as she had been, was and always would be a vital part of his!

He'd come close to trying to breach the barriers she'd put up dozens of times. But he'd always backed off. What he wanted from the woman he loved would be worthless if it weren't willingly given.

Doug stretched like a jungle cat, then sat back on his heels. He rotated his neck, trying to get a few of the kinks out. His legs seemed to have gone numb from the knees down.

Impulsively, he peeled off the paint-spattered T-shirt he was wearing and used it to mop the sweat from his chest and arms. He tossed the garment aside carelessly and looked across at his ex-wife.

Straining up on tiptoe, Amy was meticulously swabbing the upper corner of a cabinet. She was in profile, so Doug could see the movements of her small but firm breasts beneath the soft cotton shirt she was wearing. While these movements were pleasantly provocative to contemplate, they were G-rated compared with the way her very feminine derriere was displayed each time she shifted her weight. The pale pink shorts she had on fit like a surgical glove.

Slowly, Doug got to his feet. Soundlessly, he crossed to stand directly in back of Amy.

"I like your shorts," he announced.

Amy gave a gasp of surprise and dropped the sponge she was holding. It landed on the counter with a soggy plop. "D-Doug!" she exclaimed, trying to get herself turned around.

Doug grabbed both sides of the ladder, keeping it steady. By the time Amy completed her squirming maneuver, a fairly significant amount of his blood was performing a throbbing tango between his thighs.

"What—what are you doing?" she demanded looking down at him. Her eyes were very green and her cheeks were tinged with rose.

"Admiring your shorts."

"These old things?"

He shook his head. "Why is it women can't accept a compliment?"

"I'm perfectly capable of accepting a compliment, Doug. But these shorts happen to be—" she paused, appearing to calculate "—about eighteen years old. I got them in high school."

"Ah. Well . . ." Doug transferred his hands from the ladder to her hips. He felt a quiver of response run through her. "Let me be the first to tell you that you've grown into them very nicely."

Amy gave a breathy laugh and managed to ease herself down a step. This brought her face level with Doug's. She nibbled her lower lip for a moment or two, then brought one hand up and traced the line of his collarbone.

"Remember when we used to see eye-to-eye?" she murmured.

Doug cleared his throat. "I thought we still agreed on a few things."

Amy laughed again. "No, I meant when we were about the same height."

"When I was the runt of the class." Doug still recalled the humiliation of being one of the shortest boys in his grade. Lord, how he'd fought to keep up with—better yet, surpass—the "big" guys, including all three of his older brothers. In the wake of his heart attack, he'd come to realize that he'd subconsciously gone on fighting to best the "big" guys even after he'd reached his full, six-foot height.

"You were a late bloomer," Amy said comfortingly. She skimmed her palm along his shoulder, savoring his warmth and strength. Her teasing, tactile appreciation of his naked flesh made Doug catch his breath. "People have different growth rates, you know. It's all a matter of genetics and hormones."

Genetics, Doug didn't much care about. Hormones were something he couldn't ignore.

"I've got an idea," he said, genuinely surprised his voice didn't crack.

"Mmm?" Amy smiled at him.

"Let's knock off work early today. I'd like to take you out to dinner."

Seven

This was a wonderful idea," Amy said, settling into her ladder-back chair with a contented sigh. She made a brushing adjustment of the petal-hemmed skirt of her peach-colored dress.

"I thought you'd like it," Doug replied, giving her a very male look.

Amy responded with a faintly flirtatious smile, then lowered her gaze demurely. She studied her ex-husband through her lashes for a few luxurious moments. He was extremely distinguished in a classic navy blue blazer, white shirt, burgundy silk tie, and gray flannel trousers. The touch of silver at his temples gleamed.

He looked quite, quite different than he had just a few hours before. Yet as potently appealing as the transformation into self-assured sophisticate was, it was the memory of the bare-chested, blue-jeaned man who had invited her to dinner that sent a sweet shiver cascading through her.

The feel of his palms pressing possessively against her hips as he'd steadied her on the ladder . . .

The sight of his eyes growing dark with pleasure as she'd surrendered to the temptation to stroke his broad, smoothly muscled shoulders . . .

The sound of his voice invoking her name as he'd caressed her mouth with his own . . .

Restless, and fully aware of the reasons why, Amy shifted in her chair and began to glance around. She and Doug had been seated in the larger of the establishment's two dining rooms. It was a lovely setting, done up in ivory, moss green and touches of Wedgwood blue. The dining room connected to a screened-in terrace that was used for dancing. A quartet of musicians was already in place and playing.

While it was still relatively early in the evening, most of the linen-draped tables in the room were occupied. Those that were still empty bore discreetly lettered signs reading "Reserved" as well as ginger-jar vases filled with fresh flowers.

"I'm amazed we could get in on such short notice," Amy commented, patting her coiffure with fingers that weren't completely steady. She'd adopted a new style for the evening, clipping her hair back off her face with a pair of small, antique ivory combs. "I thought this place was always booked up weeks in advance."

"Vee haff our vays, fräulein," Doug answered. He was aware that the guttural huskiness of his voice was not simply due to the mock-German accent he'd adopted. He'd seen the tremor in Amy's hand and caught a glimpse of shimmering heat in her hazel eyes before she'd brought her lashes down. He understood and savored the meaning of both.

"Oh?" she challenged lightly. "Murder, blackmail or bribery?"

Doug lifted his brows. "I'm a duly constituted officer of the court, Amy," he said, substituting a rather stuffy tone for the previous Teutonic inflections. "You know lawyers never do anything illegal."

"Oh of course not, Doug," she agreed gravely. She paused to take a sip of the California White Zinfandel he had suggested they drink with their meal. The crisp yet slightly fruity taste of the white wine lingered deliciously on her tongue. "There's no such thing as insider trading on Wall Street, either."

"And if I believe that, you have some wonderful ocean-front property in Idaho you'd like to sell me, right?" He, too, took a drink of wine.

Amy laughed, causing the delicate pearl-and-coral drop earrings she was wearing to dance. The earrings matched the multistrand necklace that circled her slender throat. She had inherited the set from her mother.

"Come on," she coaxed. "Tell me how you got a reservation on such short notice."

"Would you believe I turned on the charm and seduced the reservation clerk?"

"I might if I hadn't noticed that the clerk's name is Hugo. He looks like he used to play goalie on a hockey team."

Doug pulled a frown. "Was there a compliment buried in that remark?"

"Could be. Now, come on."

"All right. All right. Lord, I'd hate to face you on cross-examination! To tell the truth, I used family connections."

"Family connections?"

"The owner of this place is one of my father's clients." Doug did not add that the owner was about to become a client of *his* as well. "I called this afternoon and dropped Dad's name."

"Oh. I see."

Their waiter arrived just then. He presented their starting courses with the air of a man who approved of what he was serving.

"The consommé with wild mushrooms for the lady," he announced. "And the vegetable terrine with coriander for you, sir." He carefully poured a bit more wine into each of their glasses, then surveyed the table. Apparently satisfied with what he saw, he nodded. "Please enjoy your meal," he said politely and moved away.

"My, how your tastes have changed," Amy remarked teasingly, nodding at Doug's terrine. Shimmering in a light coating of aspic, it looked more like a Byzantine mosaic than an appetizer. "I remember when you used to react to vegetables the way..." She searched for an appropriate comparison.

"The way Superman reacts to kryptonite?" Doug suggested.

"Close enough."

"There's a perfectly rational explanation for my aversion. I was frightened by my mother's notorious Lima Bean Surprise at a very early age. It took me a long time to get over the trauma."

"Lima Bean Surprise?"

"If you ate it and survived, you were surprised. I think it was banned by the Geneva Convention the year before I met you."

"That's not very nice, Doug," Amy chided. She sampled her appetizer. The combination of the rich taste of the Madeira-spiked chicken consommé and the woodsy flavor of the mushrooms was absolutely delectable.

"Neither is Mom's cooking," Doug responded wryly. "I love her dearly, but the woman's a menace to humanity when she's in the kitchen. You've eaten at my folks' house enough times to know that, Amy."

Amy really couldn't argue with the point he was making. Beth Browne could do a great many things. Cooking well was not one of them. Still Amy felt impelled to say something positive. "I liked those gelatin salads she used to make," she volunteered.

"You mean the moldy things with the tiny marshmallows and the maraschino cherries?"

"Molded things. Not moldy."

"Hey, you never saw one of those salads after three weeks in the refrigerator," he quipped. "But you're right. They're definitely one of the more edible items in Mom's culinary repertoire.'' Doug took a bite of his terrine, chewed and swallowed. ''You know, back in my runt days I was convinced I was short because I was malnourished.''

Amy smiled. ''I remember that history class where Miss Petty talked about the diseases sailors used to get during long ocean voyages.''

''Scurvy and rickets. I was positive I had both of them. If not, I figured there had to be a couple of dwarfs lurking around in the family tree. Of course, the fact that Larry, Scott and Jack were above average height tended to cast some doubt on that possibility.'' Doug shook his head. ''God, I really hated the way they towered over me!''

''They're a lot older than you,'' Amy pointed out. She knew that Scott, who was closest to Doug's age, was eight years his senior.

Doug ate another bite of his terrine, enjoying the subtle interplay of tastes and textures. ''I don't suppose it was easy having me running after them all the time,'' he reflected aloud after a few moments. ''Larry swears the first complete sentence I ever said was 'Wait for me!'''

''But they never did.''

''No, they never did,'' Doug affirmed, shrugging. ''So I learned to run faster. And eventually I caught up with them.''

''And won about thirty track-and-field trophies in the process.''

''Thirty-two,'' he amended, then grinned. ''But who's counting?''

Amy gave him a sassy look. ''You, obviously.''

''Well—'' Doug gestured. He didn't suppose he'd ever completely conquer the need to count his victories and compare himself with those around him. Keeping score was part of his nature. But he'd come to realize that a man could rank near the top of the tally in terms of salary and professional status, and still be a loser at life.

''Do you still have any of them?''

"The trophies? Yes, as a matter of fact. They're stashed away in a bunch of cardboard boxes in my folks' basement. My mother says she's going to unload them on me now that I have my new place."

"You've certainly got plenty of space for them."

"Is that a subtle way of reminding me that my furniture situation is a little spartan at the moment?"

"Well, there's minimalism . . . and then there's empty."

Amy wondered briefly if Doug would be willing to accept a few suggestions about furniture. While he'd been very receptive to all her decorating ideas thus far, she didn't want to press. At the same time, she was wary of getting any more involved with the restoration project than she already was. She knew that she was becoming too attached to a place she was going to have to say goodbye to in less than two weeks.

There was a brief pause. Doug drank some wine, watching Amy over the rim of his glass. A hint of sadness had descended on her, shadowing her face like a fine lace veil. He didn't know its source, but he wanted to dispel it. Sadness was not an emotion he wanted his ex-wife to feel this evening.

"What about all *your* awards?" he questioned curiously. "You must have a truckload of academic prizes—plaques, certificates, that kind of thing."

Amy shrugged. "I didn't save any of them."

"You didn't?" Doug was surprised. He knew how hard Amy had worked in school. Harder than she'd had to, he'd sometimes thought, given how naturally bright she was. "Why?"

"Oh, they didn't really seem that important. I mean, it was nice to get them, but . . ."

Letting her voice trail off, Amy dipped her head and spooned up the remainder of her consommé. She wasn't particularly comfortable with this topic. Her friend, Naomi Pritikin, had once accused her of having a "Groucho Marx" attitude about her achievements. When she'd asked what that meant, Naomi had reminded her of the great comedian's pungent quip about not wanting to join any club that would be willing to have him as a member.

I swear, that's your philosophy of life, Amy, Naomi had declared with characteristic directness. If anybody else did the things you did, you'd think they were great. But, because you do them, you think—eh, no big deal.

"I'll bet your father has at least a few of your awards put away someplace," Doug suggested after several seconds.

Amy put down her spoon. "I doubt it," she answered. "My father doesn't think they should give prizes to people for doing what they're supposed to do."

Before Doug could follow up on this bald assertion, two things occurred. The first was the return of their waiter, who swiftly cleared their table and served their entrees. The second was the arrival of three formally clad teenaged couples, whose entrance into the dining room coincided with the waiter's departure.

"My God . . ." Doug murmured wonderingly, staring across the room. He felt himself being catapulted back to another June night nearly two decades before. "Will you look at that."

Amy turned her head, following the direction of his fascinated gaze. A soft, slow explosion of surprise shook her. The present blended with the past like sugar dissolving into water.

"Prom night," she whispered.

"Has to be," Doug agreed feelingly.

He experienced a pang of nostalgic sympathy as he saw one of three youths grimace, then slip a finger inside his obviously uncomfortable shirt collar and give a tiny tug. Doug could vividly recall how constricted he'd felt on his prom night. Between the bow tie, French cuffs and cummerbund, he'd been trussed up like a Christmas turkey. But that discomfort had been minor compared to the physical pain he'd experienced when he'd gotten his first look at Amy as she'd come floating down the stairs in her prom gown.

Her hair had been longer then, tumbling below her shoulders in soft waves. Her high-waisted dress had been creamy white and moved over her slender figure like a mist. She'd worn pearls in her earlobes and around her throat and a corsage of blush-pink roses on her left wrist.

Doug's body stirred and hardened in response to an image that had stayed fresh in his heart and soul for nearly twenty years. Fortunately he now had a tailor who was more generous with in-seam measurements than the man who'd fitted him for his first rented tuxedo had been.

Amy was still transfixed by the sight of the three teen-aged girls maneuvering their long gowns and high-heeled evening sandals. They were so pretty, so obviously proud of the power of their fresh femininity. But Amy knew that underneath the satin, sequins and apparent self-confidence, there probably was a desperate fear of tripping on a hem or ripping a seam or spilling something on a dress that had taken weeks to select.

She remembered how she had felt coming down the stairs from her bedroom to meet Doug on the night of their senior prom. She'd gripped the railing so tightly, it was a wonder she hadn't left nail marks in the wood. She'd been utterly convinced that each step would turn into a stumble and that the evening she'd dreamed of for months would end in disaster before she got out the door. But somehow everything had gone wonderfully, wildly right.

Finally Amy turned back to face Doug. "Did you know?" she asked.

"What? That it was prom night?"

She nodded.

He shook his head. "No. Sandy mentioned something about having a big date this week the last time I talked to him, but I never made the connection."

"Seeing them brings back a lot of memories, doesn't it?"

"It certainly does."

Brilliant blue eyes held smoky gray-green ones captive for several long seconds. Then without looking away, Doug felt for his wineglass. His fingers closed around the fragile crystal stem. He raised the glass toward Amy.

"To prom nights . . . past and present," he proposed.

The spotlight intensity of his gaze sent prickles of awareness scurrying just beneath the surface of Amy's skin. After a moment's hesitation, she picked up her own wineglass and raised it toward him.

"To prom nights . . . past and present," she accepted.

Amy knew it was much more than a toast.

"I've been remiss tonight," Doug said as they finished their desserts.

"Have you?"

"Mmm-hmm." His eyes caressed her face like a spring rain, bathing her with a look of appreciation that made pleasure blossom deep within her even before he voiced what he was thinking. "I haven't told you how very beautiful you are."

Amy's right hand fluttered up to the base of her throat, her fingertips touching the strands of her necklace. "Thank you."

"I also haven't told you how much I want to hold you in my arms."

Amy's lips parted in a quick rush of air.

Doug smiled and inclined his dark head toward the terrace. "Would you like to dance?"

It had been a long time since they'd danced together. Amy couldn't even remember the last time they'd done so. Yet, when Doug drew her close against him, it suddenly seemed as though the last time they'd danced together might have been just a day—just an hour—before.

Their bodies moved in a harmony that was half innocent, half erotic. Their steps mated and merged with unthinking smoothness.

The quartet was playing a melody that Amy dimly associated with lyrics involving moonlight and magic. The tune could have been a commercial jingle or the Kalamazoo College fight song for all that it mattered. The moment was an enchanted one, and nothing could break the spell.

Amy sighed softly, resting her head against Doug's shoulder for a few seconds. She felt his hand tighten against her waist, heard the sharp catch-release of his breath. A warm rush of air ruffled her hair.

Doug said her name in his heart and head. Then he finally whispered it aloud, turning his mouth into the silky strands of her hair as he spoke. He inhaled deeply. The heady, feminine scent of her hazed his brain like an exotic and addictive drug.

He stroked his fingers against Amy's supple spine and felt a quiver of response. Her slender body relaxed for a melting instant in a tantalizing evocation of the much more profound yielding Doug knew would be his before the evening was over.

The quartet segued into a faster melody. Amy and Doug eased back from each other, still moving in perfectly matched partnership. After about a minute, she lifted her face to his. Her eyes were bright, her cheeks were becomingly flushed and her soft lips were curling upward just a tiny bit.

"I like your perfume," Doug said.

The curling at the corners of Amy's mouth became the kind of smile Eve might have offered Adam along with the apple. "That's why I'm wearing it."

Doug chuckled, deep in his chest. "Are you wearing anything else I might like?"

Amy's laughter was as bewitching as the look in her eyes. "You'll never find out here."

Doug brought the BMW to a halt and killed the engine. Undoing his seat belt, he turned toward Amy. Although the secluded spot he'd chosen to park had no streetlights, he could see quite clearly. There was a full moon in the cloudless, dark-velvet night sky, and it filled the interior of the car with a soft, silvery glow.

Amy unfastened her own seat belt. The clicking sound of the buckle's release seemed very loud. After a second, she turned to her left, the diaphanous fabric of her dress rustling against the silk of her stockings.

"Lovers' Lane?" she asked, tilting her head and arching her brows. She'd figured out where Doug had to be heading long before they'd gotten there. What she hadn't figured out was whether she thought his decision to go there was romantic or ridiculous . . . or both.

"Do you think it's changed much?"

Amy glanced around. "Truth?" she asked with a little laugh.

"Truth."

"I never really noticed what it looked like before."

Doug's teeth glinted as a provocative smile transformed the planes and hollows of his face. "Always had your eyes closed, hmm?"

"Not . . . always." The second word came out low and honeyed. "I just didn't pay much attention to what was outside. Plus—" She dangled the syllable.

"Plus?"

"You can't see a lot through steamed-up windows."

"Good point," he said, easing himself to the right.

Amy edged back slightly, surreptitiously checking to see that the door on her side was locked. She saw Doug's teeth flash white again and knew that he, too, was remembering the long-ago necking session when an insecurely closed door had suddenly swung open, sending the two of them toppling out onto the ground.

"Give the man an inch and he'll take the whole front seat," she observed breathily.

Doug laughed and eased even closer.

Amy ran her tongue over her lips. The slight sheen of moisture she left behind made her mouth glisten with an invitation that was as old as time. Doug's body stiffened with a response of ageless acceptance.

"You drive me crazy when you do that," he told her huskily.

"Do what?" She touched her tongue to her lips again.

"That." They were bumping knees now. "Do you have any idea what it makes me want to do?"

The moonlight had bleached most of the color out of his face. Even so, Amy could see a flush of arousal on the high, hard line of his cheekbones. His eyes looked mysteriously dark and depthless.

She smiled very, very slowly. "Why don't you show me?"

Amy and Doug had exchanged kisses—teasing, testing kisses—many times during the past week and a half. But the time for teasing and testing was over.

Doug's lips claimed Amy's with a fierce hunger. He feasted on what was offered, then sought and found the softer depths of her mouth with his tongue. He felt her hands glide up his arms, over his shoulders, then lock behind his neck. Her fingers tangled deep into his hair and she returned his kiss with a fevered sweetness.

Amy arched, trying to bring herself nearer to him. Doug seemed to understand what she was seeking. His arms tightened briefly and he lifted, settling her intimately in the hard cradle of his lap. Amy shifted her weight and heard him groan. She nipped delicately at his lower lip, then soothed the place where her teeth had touched with her tongue. He made another, harsher sound, this one torn from deep in his throat.

Amy slipped her right hand around to the front of his tautly corded throat, fumbling with the knot of his silk tie. She felt it loosen, then give way. She pushed the narrow strip of material aside and began plucking at the top buttons of his shirt.

"Oh, sweet . . ." Doug shuddered as Amy moved against him. He slid his left hand between them, stroking up until he could cup one of her breasts. He covered it with his palm, feeling the taut bud of her nipple strain against the fine fabrics of her dress and lingerie. He molded her through her clothes with gently kneading fingers, rubbing his thumb over the delicate peak that so obviously yearned for his touch.

"D-Doug!" Amy gasped on a sudden intake of breath.

She managed to pull his shirt halfway open, then insinuated her hand beneath the fine cotton to savor the sleek heat of his skin and the cut-velvet roughness of his chest hair.

Bending her head, she kissed her way down to the base of his throat, lingering for a few dazed seconds at the hollow she found there. The male musk scent of his skin filled her nostrils. The sledgehammer force of his pulse beat against her questing lips.

"Amy...oh..." His muscles clenched in a convulsive surge of pleasure and he closed his eyes. Blindly, Doug tugged at the skirt of Amy's dress, easing the fabric upward. He traced the curving line of one of her legs from calf to knee, from knee to upper thi—

The shock of realizing that Amy was wearing stockings and a garter belt, not panty hose as he'd assumed, made Doug open his eyes. The shock of having someone—or something—shine a blindingly bright light straight into his face a split second later made him shut them again.

"What the hell—?" he gasped, going rigid.

"Doug?" Amy asked bewilderedly, raising her head to look at him. She was trembling. Most of her hair had worked free of the restraining ivory combs. It swung forward to veil part of her face. She started to brush the tangled strands out of the way, then recoiled violently as a beam of illumination drilled into her eyes.

"All right, all right. Break it up in there," a gruff male voice commanded from outside the car. "This is the police. I want you two lovebirds to step out of this vehicle and show me some ID."

Eight

Jimmy Bergstrom," Doug mused nearly an hour later, pronouncing the name as carefully as he would handle a primed grenade. He shook his head and drummed his fingers on the steering wheel of his car. "Jimmy...Bergstrom."

"That's Deputy Sheriff J.W. Bergstrom to you," Amy said, struggling to put a cork in the semi-hysteria that kept threatening to fizz up her throat and out her lips. She and Doug were parked on the gravel driveway of his new house.

Doug turned his head to look at her, his expression rueful. She saw the corners of his sensually shaped mouth twitch. The tiny movement told her that as aggravated as Doug obviously was; he was still capable of appreciating the utter absurdity of what had occurred.

"I knew he'd become a cop, of course," he commented, running his fingers through his dark, disordered hair. "But the last time I saw Jimmy—make that Deputy Sheriff J.W. Bergstrom—he was working in Chicago. That was ... God! Back at our fifth high-school reunion."

"Did you recognize him right away?" Amy asked curiously. She hadn't had a clue about the identity of the officer who'd interrupted them so unceremoniously until he'd flashed his badge and announced his name. Even then it had taken her nearly a minute to accept the truth.

Doug grimaced and shook his head. Considering the condition he'd been in once he and Amy had untangled and gotten out of the car, he probably wouldn't have recognized the Statue of Liberty.

"He's gained a lot of weight," he noted after a few seconds.

"And lost a lot of hair," Amy added. The memory of the way the moonlight had bounced off Jimmy's—er, J.W.'s—balding pate made her start to giggle. She bit the inside of her cheek in what she knew was a futile effort to control the idiotic tee-hee-hee sound.

"Do you find something amusing about what happened, Amy?" Doug asked. Although his expression was sternly dignified, there was a suspicious tremor in his voice.

She met his affronted gaze with a wide-eyed look. "Umm-hmm," she said candidly, then lifted her brows. "Don't you?"

The corners of Doug's mouth twitched again. "Can I plead the Fifth?"

"Nope." She shook her head decisively.

"Temporary insanity?"

"Uh-unh."

"Nolo contendere?"

"Oh, come on, Doug!" Amy started giggling again. "Admit it! It was hi-hee-hee-hilarious. Humiliating, but h-hilarious."

Doug's lips twisted into a crooked smile. The skin at the outer corners of his eyes crinkled. "Okay. I admit it."

"And someday...we'll look back on what happened and l-laugh."

"Why wait that long?" he challenged, and began to chuckle.

The sounds of their mutual merriment filled the BMW for several minutes after that. Amy thought Doug's laughter was rich with intriguing complexities, like an expensive cognac. He thought hers was as light and bubbly as vintage champagne.

"You know..." she began after their hilarity had finally run its healing course. "You were very gallant back there, Doug."

"Gallant?" There was a lock of hair clinging to the side of her face, the ends curled in toward the corner of her mouth. Doug gently brushed it back into place. He allowed his fingers to linger briefly on the sensitive rim of her ear.

"You k-kept—" Amy's voice caught in her throat and she shivered in response to his delicate caress. "You kept trying to prevent Ji—J.W.—from getting a good look at me."

It took Doug a moment to figure out what she was talking about. "Oh, you mean when we got out of the car," he murmured.

Thinking back, he realized his actions during those first few minutes had been totally instinctive. He'd had a gut-level desire to do a great many things, including commit a couple of felonies. His primary desire, however, had been to shield Amy.

Doug knew himself well enough to accept the fact that this desire had not been sparked by altruism alone. Possessiveness, piercing and primitive, had been the main goad. He would have been damned before he'd have allowed another man to see Amy—*his* Amy—looking the way she had when he'd helped her out of the BMW. For the first time in his life, he'd understood why some men demanded their wives dress in head-to-toe veils.

The sudden fierceness in Doug's expression triggered a very elemental quiver of femininity in Amy. Reaching out, she stroked the tips of her fingers against the wedge of tanned skin laid bare by his still-unbuttoned shirt.

"Doug?" she questioned softly.

He captured her teasing hand with one of his own and pressed it flat against the spot above his heart. He looked deep into her eyes.

There was no need for him to ask.

There was no need for her to answer.

Doug's fingers weren't steady when he tried to unlock the front door to his house. Amy remembered that they had trembled eighteen years before, too, when he'd tried to insert a key into the knob of a motel room that had been rented to Mr. and Mrs. Douglas M. Browne for forty-two dollars in cash.

She heard him mutter something about "déjà vu" and smiled, knowing that the tide of memory tugged as strongly at him as it did at her.

Amy felt no uncertainty about what she was going to do. But when she saw Doug pause in the act of opening the door and go very still, she suddenly wondered if he did.

"Doug?" she asked, putting her fingers on his arm. "What is it?"

He turned to look at her. "Eighteen years ago I promised I'd protect you, and I did," he said quietly. "Taking care of you is as important to me tonight as it was back then. So if you need—or *want*—me to take precautions, I will."

In that moment, Doug seemed as much the untried boy he'd once been as the experienced man he now was. And in that moment Amy knew she loved and trusted both the boy and man without reservation.

There was no reason for Doug to take precautions, and Amy told him so.

She also told him that his promise of protection was as important to a thirty-five-year-old woman as it had been to a seventeen-year-old girl.

The inexorable passage of time had altered Doug's appearance a great deal. Amy had been aware of the changes.

She'd mapped and memorized most of them with her eyes and hands and mouth. Still, the profound differences between prom nights past and present made her regard her ex-husband almost as a stranger as the two of them stood, face-to-face, in the middle of his moonlit bedroom.

He'd shed his jacket and shirt, his shoes and his socks. Whether Amy had helped or hindered him as he'd begun to undress, she couldn't say for sure. She only knew that she'd been so hungry to touch him anywhere—*everywhere*—that the clumsiness of her fingers hadn't seemed important.

She couldn't remember what had happened to his tie. She suspected it probably was somewhere in his car, along with one of her pearl-and-coral earrings, her pearl-and-coral necklace and both her antique ivory hair combs.

None of that seemed very important, either.

"Touch me again, love," Doug invited huskily.

Amy stroked her hands up the front of his torso, recording the rippling play of his muscles with her palms. She winnowed through the coarse silk of his chest hair. There were a few, just a few, silver threads among the dark brown strands.

Doug had been in the middle of a desperately wanted growth spurt eighteen years before. The upward surge toward his eventual six-foot height had left his wiry runner's body attenuated to the point of skinniness.

The lines of his physique were still lean and taut. But he was a good forty pounds heavier than he had been. Yet not an ounce of the weight gain had gone to superfluous fat.

Amy tilted her head back so she could look up into Doug's face. Smiling with provocative promise, she sought the stiffened knots of his male nipples. She claimed each of them with caressing fingertips, inscribing circles closer and closer around the tightly furled buds of flesh until Doug groaned and imprisoned her hands with an iron grip.

"Witch..." he gasped.

Before she could say a word, Doug bent his head and took her mouth. It began as a nuzzling, nibbling, nurturing kiss.

For endless, electric seconds, he brushed his lips back and forth against hers, skimming off the sweet responsiveness his caresses were summoning to the surface.

Then with tantalizing deliberation, he began to deepen the intimacy of the kiss. At the same time, he slid Amy's still captive hands upward until her slender fingers curved and clung to the flesh of his shoulders. He felt her rise up on tiptoe, bringing herself closer in a movement that was half surrender, half supplication... all seduction.

Heat and hunger prowled through Amy like a cat—there was a sleek velvet purring one moment, a slash of claws the next. She moaned as the hard, slightly serrated edge of Doug's front teeth closed on her lower lip with exquisitely calibrated care. She moaned again as he licked the spot he'd just bitten.

She opened her mouth fully to the gliding penetration of his tongue. After a few dizzy moments, she answered the lure of his rhythmic foray and retreat. She gave herself up to the temptation of the tastes and textures of him. The line between receiving his kiss and returning it was blurred... then obliterated.

By the time Doug finally lifted his mouth from Amy's, his breathing was harsh and hoarse. "A-Amy...?" he asked raggedly.

"Yes..."

"Turn around for me, love."

"I—w-why?"

"Because... right now... I still have enough self-control to... take your dress off without ripping it." It had been more than four months since he'd touched a woman. More than four months since the night they'd made love in Chicago.

Doug watched Amy's changeable eyes grow huge as the sense of what he had said reached her. She took a shuddery little breath and bit the corner of her lip.

"Please," he said.

Amy kicked off her evening sandals and pivoted away on stockinged feet.

There were hooks and eyes at the top of her dress. It took Doug three tries to get them all undone. The urge to yank the last tiny fastening asunder was nearly overwhelming, but he forced himself not to give in.

There was a zipper, too. He dealt with that swiftly, only snagging the silk lining of the fragile garment once.

A few moments later, the dress and the pale slip Amy had been wearing lay pooled around her slender ankles like foam. A few moments after that, she pivoted back around. She was clad only in silk stockings and a few scraps of lingerie.

The inexorable passage of time had altered Amy's outward appearance in many ways. She was very obviously no longer a girl. The features of her face were more refined, more elegantly drawn than they had been in her teens. Her figure, although still very slim, was riper than it had been, as well. But these external changes were small compared with the transformation in attitude she had undergone. And essential to this transformation was the fact that on that prom night past, she—like Doug—had been a virgin.

Doug knew that the loss of physical innocence could not fully account for the profound differences between his memories of what Amy had been and the realities of what she was now. Yet he still found himself regarding his ex-wife almost as a stranger as the two of them stood, face-to-face once again, in the middle of his moonlit bedroom.

The bra she was wearing was made of ivory lace and precious little else. Her skin gleamed through the sheer material as though it had been polished with pearl dust. Doug could see the pouting crowns of her nipples very clearly. The centers of his hands tingled as he recalled the feel of those peaking rosettes pressing against his palms.

There was a dainty clasp at the base of the valley between Amy's breasts. Doug brought both hands up, undid the fastening, then brushed the lacy cups aside.

Amy whimpered as he laid claim to her now bared flesh. She arched into Doug's possessive caress, lifting her arms to circle his neck. Twisting her fingers into his hair, she pulled his head down for another kiss.

This time, she was the one who nipped and nibbled. She teased the corners of his mouth, then outlined its contours with the tip of her tongue. Her breath shattered somewhere between her lungs and her lips when his tongue came in darting search of hers, then delved between her teeth.

Doug savored the sleek, silken feel of her skin and the hot, honeyed taste of her mouth. Her inarticulate cries of pleasure were as arousing as the wild trembling of her nearly naked body.

The blood roaring through his veins was gasoline. The woman he was holding was a lighted match. Doug realized that the conflagration to come would burn down the night.

He moved his hands from the swell of Amy's breasts to the inward curve of her waist, then slipped them around to lock in the small of her back. Without breaking the seal of their kiss, he lifted her feet off the floor and carried her the few steps it took to reach his bed. Relaxing his hold, he let her body slide down against his until she was standing once again. He was rigid with need and he knew she must feel it.

Doug eased Amy down and onto her back, leaning over her, stroking her skin, smoothing her hair. She opened her eyes to gaze up at him.

"Soon," he promised.

"Now," she pleaded.

In a moment, Amy was completely naked. In another, so was Doug. She stretched out her arms to him and he went to her.

Their lips met and merged in a fierce kiss. Amy moaned into Doug's mouth...absorbing him, adoring him. She twisted, the crisp texture of his chest hair abrading the throbbing tips of her breasts.

Amy was only dimly conscious of the moment when her lover slid one of his hands down and between their bodies.

But white-hot awareness detonated in every aching cell of her being when his fingers combed through the thicket of copper-colored curls at the apex of her parted thighs and came to rest against the softly layered flesh that sheltered her sweetest secrets. She felt herself start to break apart with pleasure as he coaxed the petals of her femininity to open for him.

Doug was only dimly conscious of the moment when his lover slid one of her hands down and between their bodies. But white-hot awareness detonated in every aching cell of his being when her fingers closed around the rigid proof of his arousal. He felt himself start to break apart with pleasure as she caressed the hot, hard length that proclaimed his sex.

"Ahh . . . Doug . . ."

"Ahh . . . Amy . . ."

Doug understood with burning clarity what Amy wanted. He wanted the same thing in the same way. He was shaking with his desire for it, shuddering with a need that erupted from the very center of his soul.

He moved up, over and into her. He joined their bodies with an intimacy that was as absolute as it was inevitable. Her flesh clasped his in a caress so tight and so perfect it pushed him to the edge . . . and beyond.

"Love—" he groaned and kissed her.

Amy kissed him back, half sobbing at the exquisite sensation of being filled with such utter completeness. Ecstasy beckoned, and she moved in answer to its incandescent summons.

"Love!" she cried out as the first spasm of rapture caught her like a cresting wave.

Prom nights . . . past and present.

What had happened between Douglas Maxwell Browne and Amy Anne Hilliard eighteen years before had been incendiary despite their shared innocence.

What happened between them now was explosive because of their shared experience.

* * *

"M-m-m-m," Amy sighed, stirring with a languor borne of an utterly feminine form of satiation.

"Mmm-hmm," Doug concurred, stretching with an indolence borne of a quintessentially male kind of satisfaction.

They were lying together in a sensuous tangle of bodies and bedclothes. He was on his back. She was nestled next to him, secure in the curve of his left arm. Her right cheek rested on his chest, the crown of her head just an inch or two below his chin.

"That...was...m-m-m-m..." Amy sighed and stirred again. "I don't know..."

"Remarkable?" Doug proposed thoughtfully.

A few moments went by.

"Well..." Amy sketched a not-quite-perfect series of circles on his torso with the index finger of her left hand, enjoying the instant and unmistakable responses her teasing touch evoked.

"Amazing?" Doug suggested throatily, his voice dropping half an octave.

A few more moments went by.

"Umm..." Tongue in cheek, Amy switched to drawing figure eight patterns. She skated her index finger a little lower with each lazy loop, concentrating with Olympian intensity.

"Un—ah!—unbelievable?" Doug offered thickly. He trapped Amy's left hand with his right, effectively preventing her from progressing to more intricate designs on more intimate areas.

Amy lifted her head and surveyed him with eyes that were half smoky, half sparkling. "Actually, I think indescribable...is the word I was searching for," she informed him.

"Oh, is that what you were doing?"

"Mmm-hmm," she affirmed, then laid her cheek back against his hair-roughened chest. She smiled to herself as the rumble of his chuckle teased her ear. "Are you going to give me back my hand?" she inquired eventually.

"Not until I'm absolutely convinced you're through searching for—ah—words," Doug answered dryly, intertwining their fingers. While his voice was back to normal, his body definitely wasn't. He wanted her again. But while he knew he had the strength to satisfy himself, he doubted he had the self-control to satisfy her.

Amy snuggled nearer. "Do you think that will take long?"

"Could be." Doug shifted, savoring the feel and fragrance of her. He brushed his mouth against her hair. "Indescribable, hmm?"

"Oh, absolutely." Her tone was indulgent.

"Not . . . remarkable, amazing or unbelievable?"

"Better than that." Amy turned her face and pressed her lips lovingly to the spot beneath which Doug's heart beat. "*Much* better."

Amy drifted into a deep sleep after that. Shortly before dawn, she was coaxed out of her slumber by the questing stroke of Doug's fingers.

"Nice . . ." she murmured on a voluptuous exhalation of breath, not completely sure whether the delicious sensations spearing through her were real or part of the delightfully sensual dream she'd been having.

"Nice?" Doug challenged in a growling voice. "What happened to 'indescribable?'"

An extremely intimate touch made it explicitly clear to Amy that she was awake. "Oh . . . oh!" she gasped, moving in a purely instinctive reaction. "D-Doug!"

"That's my name," he agreed with a very male smile. "And I love to hear you say it."

Fond caresses.

Kisses. Light and sweet.

"Oh, Doug . . ."

"Yes. Just like that."

Feverish caresses.

Kisses. Long and searching.

"Doug!"

"Like that, too, sweetheart."

Doug knew every inch of her and he celebrated his knowledge with an erotic inventiveness that made Amy cry out.

Amy knew every inch of him and she cherished her knowledge with an abandon that made Doug groan aloud.

She heard herself begging him to stop, but she was afraid she would die if he did.

He heard himself urging her to go on, but he suspected it might kill him if she did.

Frantic caresses.

Kisses. Liquid and searing.

Doug gripped Amy at the waist and rolled over onto his back, shifting her so she straddled the lower part of his body. She swayed dizzily for a moment, then found her balance. Her fingers flexed once against his chest, nails biting into taut muscles for a stinging instant.

"Take me inside you, sweetheart," he whispered, kneading the curving contours of her hips and buttocks. "Take me . . . there."

Amy sighed and quivered in response to his heated touch and his hungry words. She sighed and quivered again when she felt his fingers stroke forward, then down. "Yes, yes . . ." she breathed, her answer containing both plea and promise.

Amy knelt. Warm palms molded her, callused thumbs massaged her. She shifted delicately, a starburst of desire shimmering through her. Trembling, she sought him, murmuring her satisfaction as she found the blunt rod of flesh that rose from the tangled nest of dark hair between his thighs.

"Amy." A shudder wracked Doug's body. The feel of her soft palm and slender fingers on his swollen, aching length was the sweetest form of torture in the universe. "Oh, I-love..."

He was all heat and throbbing strength in her hand. Amy stroked him lingeringly, lovingly, reveling in the potent responses she inspired. Then slowly, very slowly, she positioned herself and began to guide him within her. She sheathed him by burning increments, taking him inch by tender, tormenting inch until she had joined them as completely as he had joined them before.

Amy tilted her head back, her throat curving like the slender stem of a flower. She closed her eyes. Ribbons of pleasure unfurled inside her, twining into every part of her body. She remained still for a few electrifying seconds, then she began to rock against him. The rhythm of her movements was slow at first, but it became faster and faster, more and more urgent. She clutched at Doug with desperate fingers, her nails raking his skin with passionate demand.

Inflamed by her abandon, and all but undone by the desire she'd unleashed in him, Doug clasped Amy's hips once more. He arched up as she pressed down, driving himself deeper, deeper, into her liquid warmth. He felt the intimate quiverings of her satin flesh and knew how very close she was to finding release. He wanted that release for both of them. He stroked her again and again, her uninhibited responses making him hotter and harder than he'd ever been. His heart was hammering and his breath was coming in short, sharp gasps.

Amy repeated Doug's name over and over like an incantation until the sound of it finally fractured in her throat and became a shattered cry of ecstasy. Less than a heartbeat later, she felt his strong body clench beneath hers. She twisted herself in convulsive counterpoint, driven by a devouring need to give him what he was giving her.

Amy's last coherent thought before she surrendered the control she had always prized and protected was that what was happening between them was *not* indescribable.

It was perfect.

Nine

When Amy awoke about eight hours later, she found herself suffused with an exhilaration she hadn't felt for a long time. She was alive and full of energy. Yet the urge to jump up and greet the day was tempered by a remarkable sense of contentment.

The contentment gave way to a brief moment of confusion about where she was and how she'd gotten there. Confusion swiftly dissolved in a flood of remembered rapture. Her body hummed and heated in response to a wave of intensely pleasurable sensations.

But sensual memories could not hold at bay the stark realization that she had been left alone. Amy sat up, instinctively clutching a sheet around her. Her gaze focused briefly on the foot of the bed, which had been neatly draped with a number of intimately familiar pieces of clothing.

She opened her mouth to call Doug's name. The sound died in her throat as she froze, sniffing the air. The bedroom door was slightly ajar, and there was an alluring aroma wafting in through the narrow opening between door and frame.

Coffee?

Amy's nostrils quivered. Yes, she decided instantly. Faint as it was, the rich scent of freshly brewed coffee was unmistakable. And where there was coffee, there was bound to be Doug.

Her initial feeling of exhilaration returned. It buoyed her like a helium balloon for the next few minutes, then abruptly fizzled in the face of morning-after-the-night-before jitters when she reached the top of the stairs that led to the first floor.

What is he going to say? What is he going to do? she asked herself anxiously.

Never mind that! she decided a second later. What am I going to say? What am I going to do?

Good questions, all of them.

Amy bit her lip, pressing damp palms to the oversized terry-cloth robe she'd found hanging on the back of the door in the bathroom that adjoined Doug's bedroom. After a moment or two, she used those same damp palms to smooth back her hair.

She made up her mind. It was time to find some good answers to her good questions.

Squaring her shoulders, Amy headed down to face her ex-husband and once-again lover, Douglas Maxwell Browne.

She found him in the kitchen. He was standing with his back to her, rooting around in the depths of his refrigerator. He was crooning something that Amy thought sounded vaguely like a song about moonlight and magic.

He was also wearing nothing but a pair of faded blue jeans. The jeans looked as though they'd been cut to fit the lower part of his body with loving precision, then shrunk at least two sizes. To say the garment enhanced the anatomy it covered was an understatement.

The sight of Doug's taut, denim-upholstered rear end momentarily solved Amy's earlier dilemma about what she was going to do.

What she did was gawk at the man's backside like a moonstruck schoolgirl.

Doug sang to himself softly, promising himself that if he found the green peppers he was looking for, he could go up and check on his Sleeping Beauty—again. He also promised himself that it would be all right if he didn't hold his breath and tiptoe in and out of his bedroom this time.

He shoved aside a cantaloupe and a jar of mustard. He wouldn't allow himself to do anything as obvious as stomp across the floor, of course. But a few subtle sneezes might be acceptable.

Acceptable, yet hardly as agreeable as finally surrendering to the temptation that had been gnawing at him for more than four hours.

Doug had woken erect and ready, aching to make love to Amy again. She'd been curled against him with the innocent abandon of a kitten seeking warmth, her head tucked beneath his chin, one of her arms thrown across his torso. She'd stirred and murmured something that could have been his name when he'd shifted himself, trying to ease the lower half of his body away from hers. Her slender fingers had tightened possessively, and he'd felt the delicate bite of her nails. He'd also felt the caress of her naked breasts against his chest and the brush of her smooth thigh against his rigid male flesh. The contact had almost undone him.

God, how he had wanted her! But the serene soundness of her slumbers combined with the pricking of his conscience had kept him from taking what he so ardently desired.

And so he had lain in the bed with her, his breath sawing in and out between his teeth. He'd told himself over and over again that it was enough to hold Amy in his arms and watch her sleep. He'd also told himself over and over that this was going to be the morning when he finally offered the woman he loved the truth about himself and his new life.

At the end of ten tortuous minutes, Doug had ordered himself to get up, get out and get busy with something else. He'd known that if he remained where he was for another minute—another moment—he'd succumb to the need to peel back the sheet that covered both of them.

Amy.

Awareness of her presence reverberated through Doug, making every male instinct he had vibrate like a tuning fork. He gave himself a second to put a leash on his unruly emotions, then shut the refrigerator door and turned to face his ex-wife and once-again-lover, Amy Anne Hilliard.

Her hair was gloriously disheveled, drifting around her face like a copper-brown cloud. There was a faint flush of color on her fair-skinned cheeks, a delicate echoing of the much more vibrant rose of her kiss-ripened mouth. The expression in her wide, gray-green eyes robbed Doug of the ability to breathe for several seconds.

"Well, hello," he said finally, and opened his arms to her.

Amy went to him without hesitation, melting into his warm and welcoming embrace. The awkwardness and anxiety of just moments before vanished as his mouth came down to claim and cover hers. She reveled in the tastes and textures of his kiss, responding eagerly when he began to tantalize her with teeth and tongue.

Amy sighed blissfully when Doug finally lifted his lips from hers. She leaned back a little, secure in the support of his encircling arms. She brought her hands up and rested them lightly on his shoulders. "Good morning."

Doug chuckled and brushed his mouth against the tip of her nose. "Good afternoon," he responded.

Amy blinked. "What?"

"It's after noon," he explained, brows quirking upward. "As in, past twelve. About a quarter past, in fact."

She experienced a twinge of embarrassment—and regret—at having slept so long. "You should have woken me up," she told him after a moment. There was a faint hint of a pout hovering around her mouth.

Doug chuckled again. "Oh, I thought about it all," he drawled. He gave her a slow, sensual smile that said he'd thought about a few other things as well.

"I see," Amy responded, finding she needed to swallow between the two words. She moistened her lips with a dainty lick of her tongue and saw his eyes darken. "But after you thought about it, you decided against it, right?"

"Noooo." Doug drew the syllable out like taffy, shaking his head. Amy felt his hands gradually drift downward from her waist. His palms curved to follow the soft swell of her derriere. She shifted, and his strong fingers splayed to conform to her shape more intimately. "After I thought about it, I realized that waking you up wouldn't necessarily be the same thing as getting you out of bed." He waited a beat before adding, "Then I decided against it."

Amy buffed the hard ridge of his collarbone with the pads of her thumbs. "Too bad," she said, then sighed wistfully.

"Mmm," he agreed, caressing her through the thick, nubby fabric of the robe. *His* robe. Doug savored the idea that something he'd worn against his naked skin was now rubbing against hers. He rolled the thought around in his brain the way a gourmet might swirl a rare vintage wine over his tongue. "Of course, as any first-year law student will tell you, bad decisions can—and should—be overturned."

"But isn't the issue moot?" Amy inquired, sliding her hands around to the back of his neck. "I mean, I'm not only awake, I'm out of...mmm..."

This kiss was slower and more sultry than the first. After a few seconds, Amy sent her tongue in search of Doug's. She quivered as he met and matched her explorations with a gliding, greedy sweep of his own tongue. She drank in the flavor of him as avidly as he drank in hers.

Doug's breathing was ragged when he finally took his mouth from Amy's. Her involuntary whimper of frustration did nothing to smooth it. Nor did it help to cool the fever burning in his blood.

"Amy..." The unsteadiness of his breathing pattern roughened his voice. So did the strain of resisting his desire. Doug wanted Amy more than ever. But he knew he had to put that wanting aside and tell her the truth.

"Yes?" Amy's tone was as inviting as her expression.

"Love, I need to tell you—dammit!"

The savagely abrupt transition from confession to curse came in response to the sudden shrill of the telephone hanging on the wall next to the refrigerator. Doug's head snapped left, his eyes slewing toward the source of the mood-shattering sound. If looks could turn to lightning bolts, the phone would have been pulverized in a heartbeat.

Amy's body stiffened in instant reaction to the shrilling of the telephone, then went slack a moment later. She tightened her hold on Doug, genuinely afraid her knees might buckle beneath her. Her heart was flip-flopping inside her rib cage like a fish out of water.

One ring.

Two rings.

Three rings.

Doug brought his gaze back to Amy. She made a tiny movement of negation with her head. Ignore it, her gray-green eyes pleaded.

Four rings.

Five rings.

Six rings.

"Maybe—" Doug cleared his throat. "Maybe if you answered it, whoever's on the other end will think they've got a wrong number and hang up."

Seven rings.

Eight rings.

Nine rings.

"Oh, n-no," Amy said unsteadily, her entire nervous system jangling. "I remember what happened the last time I answered your phone."

Ten rings.

Eleven rings.

Twel—

Doug released Amy and stalked the two steps to the phone. He snatched up the receiver and shoved it against his ear. "What?" he barked.

Silence.

"What?" Doug repeated.

This time, there was a reply.

Amy hugged herself with her arms, watching Doug. Her stomach lurched apprehensively when she saw a flush of something worse than anger darken his face. His features went hard, then coalesced into a flat, expressionless mask. She had the sickening premonition that a situation which had seemed so wonderfully right only a minute before was about to go terribly wrong.

"Doug?" she questioned, barely above a whisper.

Doug looked at her with stony, sapphire eyes. "She's right here, Chaz," he said into the phone.

Chaz? Amy shook her head, not wanting to accept the implications of the name. The only *Chaz* she knew was Charles Rowand. Her employer, Charles Rowand. The same Charles Rowand who had ordered her to take three weeks of vacation.

The three weeks of vacation that were not yet over.

Doug held out the phone. "It's your boss, Amy," he told her flatly. "He says it's important."

"I'm sorry," Amy said for the seventh or eighth time. "Really, Doug."

"No problem," Doug answered tersely, giving her a variation on the response he'd already made six or seven times. "Chaz obviously wants your advice. I understand you can't give it to him without checking your files. It's a lucky thing you brought the right ones with you when you came out from the coast.''

Amy clenched her hands, tightening her fingers around the pearl-and-coral choker and earring she'd found, as she'd expected she would, when she'd gotten into Doug's BMW a short time before. She didn't think ''luck'' had anything to do with her current situation.

''I wrote an advisory memo before I left, explaining why I thought a takeover bid would be bad business,'' she said. ''Chaz asked for my input because I've had a few brushes with the CEO of the target company. I told him that while a raider like Emil Morton may look at T.W. Two Inc. and see quick profit, Tom Walker looks at it and sees his entire life.''

''You sound as though you know this Tom Walker a lot better than a few brushes' worth.'' The name was only vaguely familiar to Doug. He didn't need to ask about Emil Morton, however. The man was a corporate shark. Although he'd never had any direct dealings with him, Doug was aware that Morton had retained Allen, Chandler, Marchand and Lee on several occasions.

Amy looked at Doug questioningly. While his words sounded smooth on the surface, she heard a disturbing hint of dark depths and turbulent undercurrents. ''I . . . think I understand him pretty well,'' she said slowly. ''He's like my father in some ways.''

''Really?''

''Mmm. If he lost T.W. Two it would be, well, it would be as bad for him as it was for Dad when he finally had to retire from the bank. Do you remember what that was like?''

''I remember how much you worried about him,'' Doug replied. He also suddenly remembered how Amy had bottled up her worry and hidden it away inside herself. He took no pleasure in recalling that he'd been so preoccupied with his own concerns at the time that it had been weeks before he'd realized how deeply upset she was by her father's behavior.

Amy chewed on her lower lip for several moments. "It was so hard for Dad to let go of his work," she said reflectively. "He still hasn't. Not completely. That's the real reason he keeps putting off selling the house. He's still got an active account at the bank, you see. So when he's up here, he has an excuse to stop by a couple of times a week. It gives him a chance to see people who know who he...is." She hesitated over the tense of the verb.

"Albert Hilliard, former comptroller," Doug clarified. He felt an unexpected twinge of pity for Amy's father.

They rode in silence for the next mile or two. From time to time, Amy glanced at Doug's profile. A thick lock of hair had fallen down over his forehead. She wanted to reach over and smooth it back into place, but she resisted the urge.

She finally felt impelled to speak when Doug turned his car onto the street where she had grown from girl to young woman. "I—when I gave Chaz your number, I never actually thought he'd use it, Doug," she declared truthfully. "I just—I mean, I was spending so much time at your house—"

"You wanted Chaz to be able to reach you in case something important came up," Doug summed up. "I understand, Amy. It's fine. No problem."

Amy suddenly wanted to scream at him to stop saying "No problem" when there obviously was one, but she didn't know what would happen once she'd finished screaming, so she said nothing.

Doug pulled into the driveway of her father's house and braked the car. He looked over at her. "Do you want me to wait for you?"

"Um—" Amy rubbed her forehead with the back of one hand and met his gaze. "I don't have any idea how long this will take." The thought that she *did* know how long it would take to call Chaz, remind him she was on vacation, and then hang up buzzed through her head like a mosquito. She swatted it away quickly.

"Meaning, no, you don't want me to wait," Doug translated flatly. He folded his arms in front of his chest. He'd pulled on a sleeveless gray sweatshirt before leaving the house. The fabric of the garment stretched taut across his torso as he moved his arms.

Amy swallowed hard, feeling her body stir in response to the potent lure of his physicality. "I—I know you have things to do, Doug," she said.

For a moment, she thought he was going to get angry. More than that, she realized with shock, she *hoped* he was going to get angry. Instead he nodded curtly and snapped, "Right."

Amy sat very still as Doug got out of the car, came around to the passenger's side and opened the door for her. "Will it—will it be all right if I drive over later?" she asked uncertainly as he helped her out. The cup of his palm beneath her elbow sent a shiver of longing through her. She dropped her eyes and added, "I might as well clock a few miles on the car I rented."

Doug seemed to check himself for an instant and Amy thought she heard him catch his breath, as well. Yet when she looked up at him, his expression betrayed nothing.

"I'll be waiting for you," he answered quietly.

They walked to the front door side-by-side. When they reached it, Doug opened his mouth to speak. Amy braced herself for another trenchant comment. What she heard was a tender question.

"Do you think your father knew?" he asked her. "When I brought you home after the prom eighteen years ago, do you think he knew what we'd done?"

Amy thought back. It had been shortly before dawn when the two of them had returned to her home. They'd been holding hands. She could remember with poignant vividness how arousing even that sweetly innocent contact had seemed in the wake of what they'd shared.

Her father had reluctantly agreed to relax his usually rigid curfew in response to her pleading reminders about the long-standing senior year tradition of ''seeing in the sunrise'' after the prom. So for the first time since she'd started dating Doug, she hadn't been anxious about the hour. She'd been anxious about a few other things, however. And the issue Doug had just raised had been one of them.

''I don't know,'' she answered honestly. ''He'd waited up, but he didn't say much of anything when I came in. All he asked was whether I'd had a good time.'' She laughed a little. ''Deep down, I was sure he'd take one look at my face and know everything.''

Doug smiled, the curve of his lips rueful. ''Yeah. I figured the fact that I'd lost my virginity had to show, too. But nobody seemed to notice the transformation when I got home. My parents asked me the same thing your dad did.'' He touched Amy's cheek gently. ''I told them I'd had the best time of my life.''

She turned her face into his caress, wanting to prolong the contact. ''That's what I told my father, too.''

Doug was feeling ashamed of and angered by his earlier behavior by the time Amy returned to his house about three hours later.

What did you want her to do? he demanded of himself as he stripped and remade his bed. The sheets were redolent of the musky scent of their lovemaking. Tell Chaz to take a hike because she had more important business to take care of than his?

Yes, dammit! he answered. That's exactly what I wanted her to do!

But had you given her one reason to? Had you given her one single reason to think these three weeks are anything more to you than an extended version of what happened in Chicago? No!

I was on the verge of telling her—

Doug froze in the act of smoothing the bed's blue-and-white quilted coverlet back into place as he heard the crunch of a car's tires against the gravel driveway outside. He crossed swiftly to a window and looked out. He breathed a sigh of relief when he saw the silver-gray four-door sedan Amy had rented.

She was mounting the steps to the front porch by the time he got the front door open.

"Hi," she said, looking up at him. She was casually dressed in khaki shorts and an eggshell-colored knit top, but her manner was tense. Her forehead was slightly furrowed, and her hazel eyes were shadowed. Doug found himself remembering how she'd looked more than a month before when he'd caught sight of her walking out of the elevator of a New York City hotel.

"Hi," he responded quietly, coming out onto the porch. He waited until she'd walked up the steps, then spoke again. "Look, I'm sorry, Amy."

Her lips parted on a rush of breath. "Sorry?"

Doug nodded, hating the possible implications of the changes he detected in her. The thought that Amy might be about to announce that she was going back to Los Angeles twisted through his mind like a poisonous snake.

"Very sorry," he emphasized. "About the way I acted after Chaz called. I behaved like a—a—" He gestured, palm up, indicating that she should feel free to fill in whatever words of condemnation she deemed appropriate.

She seemed to relax a bit. And although the smile she gave him was much waner than he would have liked, Doug was glad to see it. "That's okay, Doug," she replied. "You had a right to be . . . irritated."

"I was a lot more than that," he returned.

"Oh?"

He nodded, his lips twisting. "Both of us know that sexual frustration has never done much for my temper, sweetheart."

Amy's cheeks turned pink. "Oh, well . . ."

"Even so," he added. "I was wrong to take it out on you. I apologize." He paused, trying to gauge what was going on behind Amy's gray-green eyes. "So?" he prompted after a few seconds.

Amy brushed at her hair. "So, what?"

"So, what happened with Chaz?"

"Oh. That. We, ah, talked. Then he decided we needed to conference with Emil Morton, who just happened to be flying around somewhere over middle America in his private jet." Amy shook her head, her gaze not quite focused. "You know," she mused, "there are times when I think that if Alexander Graham Bell had realized what he was letting loose on the world, he would have kept quiet about inventing the telephone."

Doug frowned. It wasn't like Amy to go veering off on tangents in the middle of a conversation about her work. "I don't see the connection," he said.

Amy blinked. "Wha—? Oh. Do you remember what you said a few weeks ago about getting away from it all? When you told me about buying this house?"

Doug saw the opening and tried to take it. "Yes," he affirmed. "Yes, I do remember, Amy. And I need to—"

"Well," she went on. "Thanks to Alexander Graham Bell and all those who came after him, we *can't* get away from it all anymore. Ever. I mean, we've got beepers and answering machines and car phones and plane phones and satellite-communication systems. God!"

"Amy—"

"In any case, Chaz eventually got the three of us hooked up. Then he put the whole thing on the speaker so his secretary could take notes. Once we got finished, I took a few minutes to take a shower, change my clothes and—" she spread her hands "—here I am. I'm sorry it took so long."

"That's all right," Doug assured her automatically, running his fingers back through his hair. "You're not going back to L.A., then?"

Amy flinched as though he'd slapped her. "No. No, of course I'm not going back to L.A. That is—" she bit her lip for a moment, then said flatly "—I'm not going back there today."

Doug realized he'd been holding his breath while he waited for Amy to answer. He released it in a rush, then told her, "I'm glad."

Ten

"Amy?"

No answer.

Doug let a minute go by.

"Amy?"

Still no answer.

Doug let another minute go by.

"Amy?"

Amy started at the sound of Doug's voice, shuddering as it broke through her confused welter of thoughts. Lifting her head, she looked to her left. Doug was about two feet away. He was stretched out on his side on the blanket they'd spread on the grassy ground about an hour before. He was propped up on one elbow, watching her. Instinct told her that he'd been watching for more than a few minutes and that he'd spoken her name several times before she'd finally responded to it.

"Sorry," she apologized quickly, curling her legs up under her.

"Is there something wrong with your grapes?" he inquired with a slight lift of his brows.

"Grapes?" she echoed blankly.

"In your hand."

"In my—" Bewildered, Amy glanced down and saw with a shock that she did, indeed, have a bunch of grapes in her hand. She had no memory of picking up the fruit. "Oh."

"Is there something wrong with them?" Doug repeated calmly.

She looked at him again. "No, no. Nothing's wrong with them." Then again, maybe there was. Maybe they'd been sprayed with some deadly pesticide. Maybe they were sour. She didn't know. "Why?"

"You've been looking at them so long, they're probably starting to turn into raisins."

"I—uh...no." Amy discarded the grapes. "Sorry. I must have thought I wanted them ... or something."

"How about some more wine, instead?" Doug suggested, nodding toward the bottle sitting on the opposite corner of the blanket along with the heel of a loaf of French bread and a small chunk of cheese. "There's still a little left."

Amy shook her head. "No, thank you. I'm fine."

No, I'm not, she thought.

No, you're not, he thought. And neither am I. Last night we were so close, our souls touched. Today, we're so far apart—

Doug shifted his body abruptly and sat up. He rubbed his palms along his denim-clad thighs. He and Amy were picnicking at the edge of the wooded area that bordered the back of the lot on which his new house was located. He'd proposed the notion of lunching al fresco shortly after her return. While Amy had been quick to accept the idea, her subsequent behavior had been distracted and disturbing.

Doug knew he had to do something. You've waited long enough, he told himself fiercely. Stop acting like a damned coward! Tell her. In the name of heaven, tell her!

"Amy."

"Doug."

They spoke at precisely the same time.

"Sorry."

"Sorry."

Again, they spoke in perfect unison.

Doug gave a humorless laugh. "We ought to work up a nightclub routine," he commented. "I seem to remember that I went first the last time this happened. It's your turn."

Coward.

About this. Yes.

Amy averted her gaze, twisting a lock of her hair. "I . . . I wasn't exactly telling the truth about not going back to L.A.," she confessed.

An icy hand grasped Doug's heart and squeezed. "No?"

Amy wrapped the strands of copper-brown hair around one finger, pulling hard enough to make her scalp hurt. After a moment, she forced herself to meet Doug's eyes. "Chaz asked me to come back early," she explained.

Tell me you want me to stay, Doug, she begged silently.

"What did you say to that?"

Tell me you don't want to leave, Amy, he pleaded without speaking.

"I said I'd talk to him tomorrow."

The late-afternoon breeze stirring the trees suddenly turned cool. A cloud slipped across the bright face of the sun. Neither Amy nor Doug spoke for several moments.

Amy adjusted her position. There was an unpleasantly familiar throbbing in her temples and she could feel the muscles in her neck tightening. She inhaled hard through her nostrils, closing her eyes and willing the pain to go away.

Doug studied her pale, set face, trying not to compare it with the flushed and radiant face he had kissed and caressed countless times before the dawn. "Headache?" he asked quietly.

Amy opened her eyes and looked at him. She felt a flash of uneasiness at her inability to hide her weakness from him.

She'd endured more than one marathon negotiating session with a splitting migraine and never betrayed her pain to a soul. But with Doug...

"Amy?" He braced himself to hear a denial.

"I do have a bit of a headache," she conceded, then scraped together a ragged laugh. "Talking with people like Emil Morton sometimes has that effect on me."

Doug relaxed a little, profoundly grateful that Amy hadn't pretended she wasn't hurting when she obviously was. "I used to be pretty good at neck rubs," he volunteered, trying to keep his tone neutral.

Amy hesitated, then gave Doug a smile which, while very small and brief, was far more genuine than her laugh had been. "I'll bet you still are."

The muscles of Amy's neck and shoulders were tense. Doug had the impression that what he was doing wasn't helping to relax them very much. But once he'd laid his hands on her again, he didn't want to take them off. The need to touch, and go on touching, was overwhelming.

Amy bit her lip, fighting the urge to melt back against Doug. She recognized that there was something irrational about resisting the comfort his ministrations could give her, but she couldn't prevent herself from doing so. He was too close and she had too many questions. She had to protect herself.

"Tell me... what you... want... Amy," Doug said into the silence that separated them. He punctuated the words with slow, kneading strokes of his fingers. He felt a sudden tremor of response run through her.

Amy took a shaky breath. Half of her wanted to turn around and look at Doug. The other half wanted to cover her face with her hands. "What... what I've got is just f-fine, Doug," she answered, striving for a casual tone and missing it by a wide margin.

"No." He shook his head, even though he knew she couldn't see him do so. "I'm serious. What do you *really* want?"

Amy arched her back and tried to ignore the panic that was clawing at her self-control, searching for a soft place to dig in...dig through. "Funny," she said after a few moments. "Somebody else asked me that very same question about a month ago."

"Oh?" Doug's tone sharpened. "Who was that?"

She wanted to tell him it was none of his business, but she couldn't. "A friend. Naomi Pritiken."

"The reporter."

Amy was surprised by his immediate placement of the name. "How—"

"You've mentioned her a couple times in the past," Doug explained.

"And you remembered."

"And I remembered." He let a few seconds slip by before ruthlessly guiding their conversation back in the direction he wanted. "What did you tell Naomi when she asked?"

Again, Amy wanted to tell him it was none of his business. Again, she found she couldn't. She could feel her self-control starting to crack. "I told Naomi...the truth," she said.

Doug's fingers stilled against the soft nape of her neck. "Which is?" he prompted carefully.

The sudden sting of tears made Amy blink. Her vision wavered and she blinked again. She pressed her palms together. Panic was no longer searching for a soft place to dig in and dig through. It had found one. "I told her that I don't know."

Doug forced his fingers to start moving again. He circled them forward a little, finding the vulnerable spot on the side of her throat where her pulse was beating out a frantic message. "I find that hard to believe, Amy," he said after a few seconds.

"What do you find hard to believe?" Amy countered, struggling to squeeze the emotions welling up inside her back into their proper places. It wasn't possible.

"That you don't know," Doug answered. "You've always been so certain about your life."

"You think so?" The retort flicked out like a knife blade before she could stop it. She heard Doug catch his breath and knew she'd hurt him.

"Yes," he affirmed, his voice steady. "I do."

I do.

He'd said those two words on their wedding day, when he'd promised to love, honor and cherish her all the days of their lives.

I do.

She'd said those two words, too, when she'd promised the same thing.

They'd both broken their promise... hadn't they?

Amy bit the inside of her lip so hard she pierced the skin and drew blood. She knew in that instant that she was going to come apart in front of him. She was going to come apart and, after so many years, Douglas Maxwell Browne was finally going to see what she was... and what she wasn't.

"Maybe you shouldn't be so certain about my certainty, Doug," she told him tonelessly.

Doug had been kneeling behind Amy, relying on the involuntary changes in her voice and body to help him make sense of what she was saying—and what she wasn't. That was no longer adequate. They were heading into a place he'd never been and he needed to look into her eyes for guidance. Swiftly, giving her no opportunity to object or resist, he shifted his body and hers and brought them face-to-face.

"All right," he said, capturing her eyes with his own and holding them steadily. "If you're not certain, what are you?"

Amy told herself she hated him in that moment, but she knew it wasn't true. Deep down inside, she was desperately afraid that she was the one she hated.

"Amy?" Doug gripped her forearms, willing her to answer him.

"I—" She swallowed convulsively.

"Tell me." He gave her a little shake.

"I—"

"Tell me. Please, love."

It was the endearment that undid her. "I'm afraid!" she burst out.

Of all the secrets in the world Douglas Maxwell Browne had thought Amy Anne Hilliard might confess, this was one of the last. "Afraid?" he repeated. "Dear God, Amy, of what?"

"Of not being good enough!" She saw a look of total astonishment come into his blue eyes. The expression ate through years of carefully constructed emotional barriers like hydrochloric acid. "Oh, you don't understand!" she cried.

"Then help me to!"

She shook her head. "It's always been easy for you—"

"Easy?"

"Yes!" She flung the word at him like a gauntlet. "Even when you were the shortest boy in class, everybody looked up to you. Everybody. Always."

"Amy—"

"It's true, Doug! And it wasn't only because you were so good at sports and school. It was because they *liked* you! They liked *you*. Even now—even now—" She gestured with both hands. "Oh, I'm not saying you've been given anything on a silver platter. I know how hard you've worked. Even though you sometimes pretend you just glide through life. You deserve everything you have. Everything. But—but it doesn't matter to you the way it matters to me. It doesn't make such a difference! You can just be who you are and it's enough. Inside, outside. It's enough. But I—" She choked, but forced herself to go on. "I have to *make* people like me, Doug. M-make them *love* me. And the only way I know how to do that is to work and work and try and try and—and sometimes, sometimes, I feel like I'm a gerbil running and running on one of those stupid roundy-roundy wheel things—''

"Amy." Doug was deeply shaken by her outpouring. Some of what she was saying he understood from personal experience. He certainly knew what it was like to be driven to run until he dropped only to realize that he hadn't gotten anywhere. But the essence of her insecurity was...dear, God! "Amy, sweetheart, liking—loving—isn't something you earn."

"Yes, it is!" she insisted wildly, balling her hands into fists and pressing them against her breasts. She was trembling like a leaf, buffeted by the force of her emotions.

"Amy—" Doug caught her clenched hands and pulled them away from her body. "Amy. Please. Listen to me. I didn't fall in love with you because you were valedictorian, a National Merit Scholar, Phi Beta Kappa or summa cum laude! And I didn't stay in love with you because you have one of the corner offices in one of the country's hottest investment-consultation firms and are pulling down a six-figure salary!"

"How do you know?" She couldn't believe him.

"Because I know!"

"But it makes a difference, doesn't it?" she demanded. "All those things you said? What I am?"

"Amy, what you *do* isn't who you are!"

"Yes, it is. *Yes, it is!*" Her voice was shrill. "And it isn't good enough, is it, Doug? No. No, it isn't! I know that. I've always known that. I'm not good enough. I've never been good enough! Even...even my fa-fath—" She stopped abruptly, jerking her hands out of his and pressing them against her lips.

Doug was torn between two extreme emotions. The first was an aching compassion directed at her. The second was a corrosive anger directed at himself. Dear Lord, how could he have claimed to love this woman with all his heart and been so blind to her vulnerabilities? No matter how skilled

Amy had been at hiding them—and she obviously had been skilled to the point of genius—she couldn't have deceived him so thoroughly without his complicity.

"What about your father?" he demanded tautly.

Amy shook her head.

"What about him?" Doug repeated. "Is he the one who made you believe you aren't good enough? Is he the one who told you love has to be earned? Is he? Dammit, tell me, Amy!" He knew in his gut that he was trying to ameliorate his sense of guilt by finding someone to blame as the source of Amy's pain. He also knew it wasn't going to work.

Amy brought her hands down a little, staring at Doug's face but seeing her past. She'd told him everything else. She might as well tell him this.

"I . . . I remember once, I came home with a . . . a ninety-six on a test," she said slowly. "An A-plus. It was . . . it was the best grade in the c-class, Doug. The very best. And I thought—I hoped—he would be proud of me. That he'd hug me and tell me I was wonderful. He . . . he looked at the test for a long time when I gave it to him. Then he said: 'A ninety-six, Amy? You got a ninety-six? That's four percent wrong, isn't it. How—how would you like to go to a s-surgeon who gets four percent w-wrong?' "

Amy felt her eyes fill and knew she was about to weep. She turned her face away, wiping at her cheeks with shaking fingers.

"Amy, love." Where Doug's voice had been savage a minute before, it was now soft. He reached out and cupped Amy's chin. She jerked away as though she'd been scalded.

"No," she said rawly. "I don't want you to—I know you hate to see me cry." This was a lie. What she truly knew was that *she* hated to have him see her cry. On the few occasions during their marriage when she'd given way to tears, she'd wept in the shower with the water running rather than have him realize what was happening.

Amy's rejection hurt, but Doug endured the pain without protest because he finally understood why she needed to hold herself aloof. And in the midst of his acceptance of the pain, there came a memory of piercing sweetness. He caught Amy's chin again and gently but inexorably made her turn her face back toward his.

"The only time I ever saw you cry was the first time we made love," he told her huskily. "And you saw me cry that night, too. I cried because of what I felt for you. What I still feel for you, Amy. What I'll always feel."

Amy shook her head. She was trapped in a cage that had been thirty-five years in the making and she could not get out. "It's too late."

Too late.

Her words reverberated in Doug's brain like a death knell. This was the fear he'd confessed to Paul Lansing. He shook his head, denying her words, denying his fear. "No."

"Yes."

"No, Amy—"

"Yes!" Her voice rose on the word, then splintered. When she started speaking again, it was in a flat, frighteningly controlled tone. "I want to go now, Doug."

"Go?" The syllable stuck in Doug's throat like a razor blade. He swallowed and was surprised he didn't start to choke on his own blood. "Go where? Back to L.A.?"

For a moment, Amy seemed to be considering it. In that moment, Doug vowed he would follow her if she said yes.

"Not...today," she said finally. "I'm not going back there today. I told you that before." Her milk-pale cheeks were glistening with tears.

"Then, where?" He took her by the shoulders, intending to hold her where she was. He intended to hold her and hug her and tell her she was wonderful over and over again until she believed him.

"To my...father's...house."

"Amy—"

"Let me go, Doug."

"I can't."

"Please."

"No. Don't go, Amy. Stay here. Stay with me."

Amy had yearned to hear him say those words. She'd *needed* to hear him say them. And now that he finally had...

"Stay and do what?" she asked.

He smoothed his palms down her arms and took her hands in his own. He raised them to his lips, kissing the right and then the left. Amy trembled once, then went still. "Whatever you want, love," he answered.

Amy tried to shape her mouth into a smile, but she understood from the anguished expression in Doug's sky-colored eyes that she'd botched the attempt miserably.

"I told you," she said numbly. "I don't know what I want."

Eleven

———

The telephone was ringing when Amy reached the front door of her father's house about twenty minutes later. She could hear it, shrilling on and on.

I can't get away from it all, she thought, her hands shaking violently as she tried to insert the key in the lock. I can't get away from anything.

She'd stopped crying when she'd gotten into her rented car to drive away from Doug's house. Her eyes were still dry, but she seemed to be having trouble focusing them.

It took Amy more than a minute to get the front door unlocked and open. The phone was still shrilling. She walked into the buff-and-blue papered foyer with her hands pressed against her ears.

Ring, ring, ring.

Maybe—maybe if you answered it, whoever's on the other end will think they've got a wrong number and hang up, Doug had suggested with a teasing glint in his blue eyes only hours before.

Oh, no, she'd answered. I remember what happened the last time I answered your phone.

Amy knew the sound wasn't going to stop. Or that if it did stop, it would soon start again. She knew these things in the same way, with the same certainty, that she knew it was Doug on the other end of the line.

She took her hands away from her ears and went to answer the phone.

"D-Doug?"

"I wanted to make sure you'd gotten home all right, Amy."

"I'm here." She wasn't home and she wasn't all right but she wasn't going to say that.

"You told me you could manage on your own."

Amy closed her eyes, acknowledging the accuracy of the quote with a pang of regret. "Yes, I did."

"I've always believed that, Amy."

"Have you?" She hadn't. So she kept on trying to prove it, over and over. Amy the Able. Amy the Independent. Amy...the woman who ached with needs that ran so deep she was terrified to admit to them.

"Yes."

Amy opened her eyes and stared at whatever was in front of her without registering a single detail of what she was seeing. "Doug—"

"I let you go because you said that was what you needed, Amy. But I...I can't leave you alone. Please."

"No!" Amy stopped him before he could voice the plea she knew would devastate her no matter how she responded to it. "I...I need to be alone, Doug. I need to be by myself. *With* myself." Whoever that self is, she added silently. "I have to think. I have to...decide."

There was a long silence on the other end. "If you decide to go back to L.A., will you tell me?" Doug asked finally. "Before you leave?"

His questions stabbed Amy like knives. Did Doug honestly think she'd leave him without a word? Did he truly think she was capable of doing something like that to him? Didn't he know her at all? Didn't he understand what he meant to her?

No, she thought painfully, maybe he doesn't. Right now, *I* don't feel as though I "know" me at all. How can I expect him to? And as for understanding what he means to me...

"I'll tell you what I decide, Doug," she said quietly. "I'll tell you... everything."

"Face-to-face."

"Wh-what?"

"Face-to-face, Amy. You'll tell me everything face-to-face. Even if 'everything' is only a goodbye."

Amy put her left hand to her throat. She realized she was rubbing her ring finger with the pad of her thumb. She made herself stop. "Yes," was all she answered. It was all she *could* answer in that moment.

"You promise?"

"I promise."

"I love you, Amy. I love *you*. Please, believe that."

"I... want to. I really want to, Doug."

Amy managed to hang up before she broke down. Shaking with emotions she couldn't catalogue because she'd never acknowledged she was capable of experiencing them, she collapsed onto her knees. Tears spilled out of her eyes and rolled down her face unchecked. She felt the hot wetness of them on her cheeks, tasted the salt of them on her lips. They dripped off her chin and ran down her neck, dampening her off-white knit top and the skin beneath.

Her throat was dry and tight and each one of the sobs that rose up into it had to be choked out. She heard the raw, rasping sounds she was making at a great distance, as though they were coming from a stranger.

Amy had no idea how long she cried. She had many years' worth of tears stored inside her, waiting to be released. The wonder—or perhaps the pity—of it was that they hadn't overflowed before this.

Eventually she stumbled upstairs, dimly registering the fact that dusk was falling outside and the house was growing gloomier by the moment. Driven by some perverse instinct, she sought refuge in the bathroom. After peeling off her clothes and casting them aside, she stepped into the tub, pulled the plastic curtain closed and turned on the shower full blast. Shuddering with grief and pain and confusion, she turned her tear-drenched face into the warm, gushing water and went on weeping.

Amy never remembered turning off the shower, getting out of the tub, or toweling dry. Her next real memory was of being hideously sick in the sink. When she finally managed to raise her head, she caught a glimpse of her face in the mirrored front of the medicine cabinet and was sick again.

Finally, there was nothing left to retch up and no more tears to be shed. Amy staggered out of the bathroom, down the carpeted hallway and into her blue-and-white bedroom. The sanctum sanctorum, Doug had called it.

She'd never known he'd fantasized about her bedroom.

She'd never known a lot of things.

She knew them now, though.

And somehow . . . some way . . .

We can't turn back the clock, she'd told her friend Naomi, repeating the words she'd said to Doug.

Would you want to if you could? Naomi had asked.

I . . . only if I could figure out what I did wrong and put it right.

Amy collapsed onto her bed. Her narrow, virginal bed where she had fantasized about Doug during more nights than she could count.

But he didn't know that.

He didn't know it because she'd never told him.

He hadn't known a lot of things about her because she'd never told him. She hadn't told him because she'd been too afraid.

And then, today, she'd finally confessed to that fear. She'd confessed to it, and she'd told Doug more about herself than she'd ever told anyone. She'd told him all the awful truths. The truths she'd always believed would destroy her if she admitted them to another living soul.

Yet, Doug hadn't seemed to think they were awful. Not in the way she did. In fact, instead of rejecting her as a fraud or a failure after he'd heard her confession, he'd reminded her of one of the most beautiful of all the beautiful moments they'd shared. He'd reminded her of the moment they'd wept together in love and joy and discovery.

And after that he'd asked her to stay with him. Having finally learned what she truly was...and truly wasn't, he'd still wanted her to stay with him. He'd told her that.

He'd also told her that he loved her. That he loved *her*.

Amy had thought she would have to cry herself to sleep. She was wrong.

Amy had thought she would have nightmares.

She was wrong about that, too.

Doug sipped at the second glass of Scotch he'd had since his heart attack. He'd finished the first glass of Scotch he'd had since his heart attack just a short time before.

He had no intention of getting drunk. He'd already committed his quota of stupid acts for the century. Deliberately getting himself plowed, plastered or pie-eyed wasn't on the agenda.

He only wanted to numb the anguish he was feeling. He was not indulging in the delusion that alcohol was going to make the pain go away entirely. He knew the most he could hope for was that the Scotch would dull the edge of the blade that was slicing his soul to ribbons.

Doug was sitting on the top step of his front porch. It was past midnight, some kind of insect kept biting him, and the only illumination in the darkness came from a dim overhead bulb. Doug didn't give a damn about any of these things. He was ready to endure a hell of a lot worse to avoid going inside again.

Amy. She was everywhere inside his house—*their* house. She was everywhere, in every way...except the one that really mattered. And the possibility that she might never be there in that way again was killing him by inches.

Why didn't she tell me?

Did you ever ask?

Why didn't I see?

Did you ever really look?

Doug closed his eyes, reviewing the hints and clues about Amy's inner self that had always been there. He *had* seen them, even without really looking. But he'd never put them together.

He'd considered himself a man on the mend in the wake of his heart attack. He'd thought he'd figured out all the mistakes that had landed him flat on his back in an emergency room, and he'd thought he knew how to correct them. He'd been so smug, so certain, so sure.

And then Amy had wept in front of him for the second time in their relationship and told him the truth about herself as she perceived it.

He'd spoken the truth when he'd told her he hadn't fallen in love with her because she'd been valedictorian, National Merit, Phi Beta Kappa and summa cum laude. He didn't deny that her intelligence and intensity attracted him, but they weren't the only qualities that made him catch his breath each time he saw her.

He'd spoken the truth, too, when he'd told her he hadn't stayed in love with her because she had one of the corner offices in one of the hottest investment-consultation firms in the country and was pulling down a six-figure salary. Again, he didn't deny the appeal of her achievements—and dammit, maybe, yes, his desire to lay intimate claim to a remarkable woman like Amy Anne Hilliard *had* once been mixed up with his need to count his victories and compare himself with those around him. But, no more. Dear God, no more.

Doug shook his head, then took another swallow of Scotch.

The truth was, he loved her. He'd thought he'd loved her in every way a man could love a woman before, but he had learned today that there were ways of loving he hadn't even known existed.

He loved her, and he'd hurt her. The fact that he'd hurt her without meaning to—by acting on the best intentions possible—didn't matter.

He'd once told himself that he wasn't arrogant enough to believe he was the sole cause of whatever was wrong with Amy. He'd also told himself that he wasn't arrogant enough to believe he could be the sole cure. He'd been lying in both instances. He had been that arrogant . . . and worse.

Doug sighed and put his glass down next to him. He had Amy's promise that she would tell him everything, face-to-face, once she'd made the decisions she needed to make...alone. He knew he would cling to that promise until they met again.

He also knew that he would cling to Amy's shattered confession that she wanted to believe he loved her. He would cling to it, and he would do anything in his power to convince her that what he'd said was true.

Amy woke shortly after ten, blinking her eyes against the golden haze of sunlight pouring in through her bedroom window. She lay still for several seconds, then sat up slowly. The bed sheet slipped away from the upper half of her body and puddled around her hips.

She felt . . . strange. Not at all like herself. She felt light-headed to the point of giddiness—as though she'd just emerged from the delirium of a high fever.

She knew she'd been dreaming. Dreaming of Doug. She'd been dreaming that she was dancing with him in a magenta, mauve- and mint-paisley ballroom decorated with huge bouquets of blush-pink roses. A quartet of Groucho Marxes clad in crisply starched blue-flowered boxer shorts had been playing a song that had something to do with moonlight and magic.

She had been smiling.

So had Doug.

She'd been saying, "I love you."

So had Doug.

Amy closed her eyes for a moment. The image returned. She opened her eyes. The emotion remained.

She'd never doubted her feelings for Doug. Not even during the times when she'd doubted everything else about herself. Even before she'd understood what they meant, the feelings Doug evoked in her had been the shining, sustaining constants in her life.

She *had* doubted *his* feelings for *her*. Not always. Not consciously. And not because of anything he'd done. No, the doubts had been hers. All hers. She'd doubted his feelings because she doubted herself.

It isn't good enough, is it, Doug? she heard herself crying. No. No, it isn't! I know that. I've always known that. I'm not good enough. I've never been good enough.

Amy caught her breath. *How* did she know? she demanded of herself suddenly. How did she know she wasn't good enough? Because her father had told her so?

All right, yes. Her father had always found reasons to carp and criticize. He'd never been completely satisfied with anything she'd done. But, sweet heaven, she was a thirty-five-year-old woman now, not a little girl! Wasn't it about time for her to start judging herself by her own standards?

And what did "good enough" mean, anyway? Scoring one-hundred percent each and every time? No one could do that!

She'd been "good enough" to graduate first in her high-school class as a National Merit Scholar. She'd been "good enough" to earn a Phi Beta Kappa key and a summa cum laude in college. She'd been "good enough" to finish in the top three at business school and she was "good enough" for mega-millionaires like Emil Morton to listen to her advice and consulting wizards like Charles Rowand to tell her she was indispensable.

Good enough? Why, if anybody else had done the things she had—

If anybody else did the things you did, you'd think they were great, Naomi Pritikin's trenchant voice echoed inside her head. *But because you do them, you think—eh, no big deal.*

What you do isn't who you are, Doug's voice countered tenderly within her heart. *And I love you, Amy.*

"But, who am I?" Amy asked aloud.

The answer came back to her like a benediction. She was Amy Anne Hilliard, the woman who loved Douglas Maxwell Browne.

She was also a woman who, finally, was ready to admit she knew exactly what she wanted, needed . . . and deserved.

The jangle of the telephone next to Doug's bed shocked him out of a troubled sleep and into a state of total alertness. He grabbed for the receiver as though it were a life line.

"Hello?" he said into the mouthpiece. The pounding of his pulse would have done credit to the entire percussion section of a symphony orchestra.

"Doug?"

The voice on the other end was familiar and well-loved. It was also briskly male.

"Hello, Dad," Doug answered after a few seconds. He raked his fingers back through his hair. "What's up?"

No answer.

"Dad?" Doug felt a ripple of uneasiness. Hearing his father's breath come out in a long hiss didn't help.

"You forgot." It wasn't a question.

"Forg—" Doug began, then broke off as comprehension hit him like a two-by-four between the eyes. He swore as a conversation he'd had with his father ten days before came back to him. "The meeting with Hardy and Peterson. Damn! You told me you'd set that up for today, didn't you." The men in question were two of his father's most important clients and until yesterday Doug had anticipated that they would be figuring in his professional life, as well.

"They're due to walk into my office about forty-five minutes from now," his father affirmed. He paused a beat. When he continued speaking, there was a touch of paternal jocularity in his voice. "They're anxious to meet you, Doug. They want to make sure my son—and soon-to-be partner—is as good a lawyer as I keep claiming."

"Dad—"

"I know, I know. It's all right. I realize you've had a lot on your mind. I meant to give you a call the other day to remind you, but I got involved in some other things. Oh, well, that's water under the bridge. If you get a move on, you've got just enough time to get yourself pulled together and drive over here. Only, for Pete's sake, watch the speed limit! You remember that friend of yours—Jimmy Bergstrom? Well—"

"He's the new deputy sheriff in town," Doug filled in. "Yeah, Dad. Amy—" He found he had to pause and swallow before he could go on. "Amy and I found that out the other night."

"He gave you a ticket, right? What was it? Going twenty-seven in a twenty-five mile zone?"

"Not exactly," Doug answered. Despite the emotional weight he was carrying, his mood lightened for a moment as he thought of his and Amy's encounter with his boyhood chum. "Anyway, he let us off with a warning."

"A warning?" Lawrence Browne repeated, palpably astonished. "Son, you must be a better lawyer than even *I* say you are! By the way, speaking of Amy. Do you think there's any chance you might get her to come to the office with you?"

"Dad—"

"I happened to mention to Max Peterson that she was in town. He knows her by reputation and he's interested in—"

"Dad!" Doug interrupted sharply. "You didn't say anything about our getting—about her coming here to live, did you?"

There was a brief silence. When Lawrence Browne spoke again, his tone was much less ebullient. "No. No, of course not, Doug. I was only thinking that with Amy's background and the kind of capital investment Max is involved with, it would be, well, never mind that. What's happened?"

"I can't . . ."

"You've finally told Amy the truth—is that it?"

Doug shook his head. "No, I haven't. But please, Dad, don't start in on that. You can't give me a rougher time about it than I've already given myself. The fact is, Amy may be going back to L.A. And if she does, I'm going after her."

There was another silence, longer than the previous one. "I see," his father returned finally. "In other words, you're saying I may not be getting a new partner, after all."

"I'm saying it's a possibility. I'm . . . sorry, Dad."

"Oh, hell, don't be sorry, Doug! You know how your mother and I feel about Amy. And you know how we felt about the two of you breaking up."

"If I remember correctly, you told me I needed a swift kick in the butt to help put my head on straight," Doug responded with a touch of bitter humor.

"Yes, well." Lawrence Browne cleared his throat. "About this meeting with Peterson and Hardy. I don't want to sound like I'm putting the pressure on, especially now. But it wasn't easy getting the two of them to come over here."

Doug had already made up his mind. "I understand, Dad," he cut in. "I promised to be there and I will."

"Thank you, Doug." The voice on the other end of the line sounded very relieved. "Oh, one other thing."

"Yes?"

"Your mother wants you to leave a key under the mat. She's coming over with a couple of boxes of your stuff."

Doug tried to reach Amy by phone five times before he left for his father's office. Each time he called, he got a busy signal. Finally he knew he couldn't delay his departure any longer.

Although he prayed Amy would not come while he was gone, he left a note tacked to his front door . . . just in case.

"Amy—" it began. "Stay. Don't leave. I need you. I want you. I love you. *You*, Amy. *You*. Please. Believe me."

He signed it: "Yours, Doug."

Amy spotted the note with her name written on it as she started up the steps to the porch of Doug's house. She recognized the boldly scrawled script instantly. The already rapid beating of her heart increased in tempo.

The front door swung open a split second before her foot hit the top step. Amy almost stumbled. "B-Beth!" she exclaimed, recovering her balance with a singularly ungraceful maneuver.

"Amy, dear!" Doug's petite, silver-haired mother greeted her with a smile so warm it put sunshine to shame. "How wonderful to see you again! I was just over here unloading some of Doug's things. Honestly, the amount of stuff he still has stashed at our place is ridiculous!"

"Doug's not here?" Amy asked quickly, trying to control her disappointment.

"Oh, he'll be back very shortly, I'm sure," Beth Browne assured her. "He's at his father's off—" She stopped abruptly, her blue eyes focusing very intently on Amy. "Something's happened, hasn't it? I can see it in your face. I'd say you look years younger than the last time I saw you, but at your comparatively tender age I don't suppose that would mean much. Still, you look quite...quite..." She gestured. "The change is almost indescribable, Amy!"

The older woman's choice of adjective inevitably reminded Amy of the heady moment, two nights past, when she'd used the same word. The memory sent a purr of pleasure through her and made her cheeks grow warm.

"Actually, something *has* happened," she started to confess, then hesitated. She'd wanted Doug to be the first to know.

"Yes? Yes? Go on, dear."

"Well," Amy laughed a little. "All right. The truth is, I just called my boss in L.A. and told him I'm quitting."

Beth Browne's eyes lit up. "You're coming back to New York!" she rejoiced, then hugged Amy. "Oh, I'm so glad."

Amy was pleased but slightly startled by the fervor of the other woman's reaction. She could only pray that Doug would greet her news as enthusiastically as his mother had. Amy wanted them to be together again, and she knew that wasn't going to happen as long as he was living and working on one coast and she was living and working on the other. It seemed only right that she be the one to make the move. Besides, she and Doug had roots in New York. They had a history there. Even the house—

"I hope you took my son to task for waiting so long to tell you everything," Doug's mother declared, interrupting Amy's thoughts.

"Tell me...everything?" Amy echoed, confused by the first part of Beth's statement.

"You have every right to be furious, if you ask my opinion," the older woman went on, apparently not hearing Amy's question. "And you really do like the house? I confess, I poked around a bit when I was inside. I can't believe the improvement! My God, when Doug showed me this place initially and said he wanted the two of you to live here, I thought he must have suffered brain damage, not a mild heart attack! And that's another thing, Amy. I begged him to let you know what—Amy? *Amy!* What's the—oh, no! You mean he hasn't told you *any* of it?''

Twelve

———

Doug wasn't certain what he'd find when he arrived at the Hilliard house about forty minutes later. But he knew that whatever it turned out to be, it wouldn't be pleasant.

He'd gotten through the appointment at his father's office as quickly as courtesy allowed. As soon as the session had begun to shift from the professional to the personal, he'd excused himself and gone to phone Amy once again. There had been no busy signal this time. Instead, the line had rung and rung and rung without a pickup.

Clamping down on a sudden surge of anxiety, he'd reminded himself of Amy's promise that she would meet him face-to-face once she'd made the decisions she needed to make. He'd hung on to that thought for dear life as he'd called his own number. But instead of reaching Amy, he'd reached his mother.

She'd been frantically upset—probably as close to hysteria as she'd ever been. Despite this, it had taken him only a few terrible seconds to make sense of what she'd been saying.

Amy knew. Amy knew *everything*.

Everything, that is, except his reasons. And he'd only come to fully understand them himself during the darkness that had preceded this day's dawn.

Doug had spared a few moments to comfort his mother as best he could, telling her over and over again that he—not she—bore the blame for what had happened. Finally she'd told him she would be all right and pleaded with him to go to Amy.

He'd needed no further urging.

The four-door sedan Amy had rented was in the driveway when Doug arrived. He breathed a silent prayer of thankfulness, then pulled in behind the vehicle and deliberately blocked its path. He was out of his own car two seconds later.

The front door to the house was ajar. He let himself in without the slightest hesitation.

There was no need to look for Amy. There was no need to call out her name. She was standing in the middle of the foyer, clutching one handle of the large leather suitcase he'd lugged across the airport parking lot for her less than two weeks before. The latches that were supposed to hold the bag shut apparently had given way. The suitcase had fallen open and half its contents were spilled out onto the polished wooden floor.

Doug absorbed the whole scene in the space of a single heartbeat, then focused his entire attention on Amy. She stared back at him, eyes huge, her face the color of typing paper.

"You promised you'd see me face-to-face before you left, Amy," he said walking toward her very slowly.

Amy let go of the handle of the suitcase, not caring that the bag thudded on the floor and disgorged what was left of its jumbled contents. She took a step backward, not wanting Doug to come within touching distance. She could see from his face that he knew she finally knew everything. Everything!

"I lied," she answered tautly. "Just like you." She saw him flinch and she wanted to be glad that she'd hurt him, but she couldn't.

Doug stopped moving and shook his head. There was about a yard between them. Instinct told him that Amy wouldn't let him come any closer. Not now. "I didn't lie to you, Amy," he said quietly.

Amy clenched her hands into fists and tried to still the trembling that had taken hold of her. She tried to choke down the question that rose to her lips, too, but it wouldn't be stopped. "Why didn't you tell me, Doug?" she demanded rawly. "Why didn't you tell me?"

For twelve mornings in a row, Douglas Maxwell Browne had gotten out of bed promising himself that this was going to be the day he told Amy Anne Hilliard the truth. The *whole* truth.

Now, at last, he fulfilled that pledge.

"I didn't tell you because I was an arrogant jackass who thought he'd gotten a peek at the master plan and figured he knew how to right every wrong, correct every mistake and make sure he and the woman he loves lived happily ever after," he said with savage precision. He saw Amy's lips part on a sudden gasp of pain. Her gray-green eyes were shimmering with unshed tears. "I also didn't tell you because I was—*am*—afraid."

Her reaction was almost identical to the one he'd had when she'd made her confession of fear to him the previous day. *"Afraid?"* she repeated. *"What are you afraid of?"*

"A lot more than I've been willing to admit to," he answered. "But the worst fear, the one that's caused the most hurt, is the fear that what you do is more important to you than I am. The fear that your work fulfills you more than I do. The fear that if I ever asked you to choose between the two, you wouldn't choose me."

Amy looked at him, not believing what she had just heard. Doug—*afraid*? Afraid of losing *her*?

Dear God, she thought in horror. Naomi was right! That day at brunch—she was right!

"Was that—" Amy could hardly bear to voice the idea, but she knew she must. "Was that why you never raised the possibility of my turning down the job in Los Angeles? Because you thought it might mean more to me than you?" she asked in an aching voice.

Doug nodded.

"And you didn't—you didn't tell me you wanted me to c-come back to New York and l-live with you and be your w-wife again because you thought I'd rather stay in L.A.? Because—because of my career?"

He nodded again.

"And when...and when you h-had your heart attack—?"

"Part of it was stupid male pride," Doug said, forking his fingers back through his hair. "I didn't want you to see me flat on my back, Amy. I felt so damned weak. So vulnerable."

"Oh, Doug."

"But the biggest reason I didn't want you to know what had happened was fear."

Amy took a step toward him. She couldn't help it. "Fear that I wouldn't come to you if I knew, Doug?" she asked, her throat tight. The realization that Doug had formed this impression of her was painful in the extreme. But the recognition that she had given him reason to form it was devastating.

Doug didn't say anything. He couldn't. Not at that moment. The anguish in Amy's eyes made it impossible for him to speak.

"I felt it, you know," Amy told him after a moment. She brought her hands up and pressed them, one on top of the other, against her breast. "I felt your heart attack."

"*What?*"

"I felt it when it happened," she said. She'd pried enough details from Beth Browne to piece the scenario together. "At the exact moment you were having your heart attack on a squash court in New York, I was waking up in a Tokyo hotel room in a panic, feeling as though . . . feeling as though someone was trying to crush my chest. And I had this . . . this awful conviction that something terrible had happened to you."

Doug was stunned. So many of his thoughts while he'd lain on the squash court had been of Amy. Could he possibly have—could she have felt him crying out for her from half a world away?

"I didn't know," he whispered, grappling with the implications of what she'd said. "Amy, I didn't—" Something clicked into place. "Is *that* why you called Margaret at the office that day?"

Now it was Amy's turn to nod.

"She said you didn't sound like yourself. She didn't know about the heart attack, Amy. Not then, at any rate. And afterward—"

"And afterward, you told her not to tell me anything. Just the way you told your parents."

"I—"

"Why didn't you have someone call me, Doug?" Amy cried. "Why?"

"You were on the other side of the world—"

"I could have caught a plane!"

"There was nothing you could have done!"

"N-nothing?" Amy almost choked as she finally swallowed the bitterest truth in the universe. "That's not really it, is it, Doug? You didn't call because you thought I'd stay in Tokyo, even if I knew you were sick!"

"You were on the verge of closing the biggest deal of your career, Amy! The night we were together in Chicago, you couldn't stop talking about it. How could I—"

"Deal?" Her voice cracked. "Career? God, Doug! You *needed* me, and I wasn't there for you!"

"I needed you before my heart attack, Amy," he answered. "And you weren't there for me then, either." He watched her sway as though he'd struck her. It tore him apart to see the pain he was inflicting, but there was no other way. He closed the gap between them with one long stride and caught her by the shoulders. Amy flinched against his hands. "And there were plenty of times when *you* needed *me* and I wasn't there for you," he told her fiercely.

"What?"

He repeated his assertion.

"N-no—" Amy tried to deny it, even as she saw the truth of what he was saying.

"Yes, dammit!" he insisted. "Yes, love. It's true. If I'd been there for you when you needed me, you never would have ended up crying that you aren't good enough! If I'd been there for you, you would have realized a long, long time ago how very special you are—no matter what your father told you when you were growing up."

There was a long moment of silence. Amy felt everything start to tilt. But not out of line. No. She had a sudden sense of her life moving into balance for the first time ever.

"Doug—" She knew she was on the brink of a tremendous discovery. All she had to do was have enough faith in herself to take the necessary steps forward to reach it.

Doug tightened his hands, staring deep into her eyes. "Don't you see, Amy?" he said softly, persuasively. He was speaking from the heart and he was telling her nothing but the truth. "Don't you see? We found each other in fourth grade. *Fourth grade!* We went from friends to lovers to husband-and-wife. And it was so good. It was so *easy*. We hardly had to work at it, did we? So we worked at everything else. We became the perfect fast-track couple. We had our eyes on the glittering prize. Me, trying to prove I could beat the big guys. You, trying to prove you were good enough. We were so busy reaching for the top that we didn't see we were letting love slip through our fingers."

"It . . . wasn't what we *did*," Amy said slowly, understanding breaking over her like a sunrise. And with that understanding came courage and hope. "It was what we *didn't* do."

Doug nodded. "We worked together to build a beautiful relationship, and then we didn't take care of it."

The word build triggered a connection in Amy's mind. The house. Doug's house! "You . . . you're saying we neglected each other."

Doug saw the expression in Amy's eyes change and knew what she was remembering. "Yes," he agreed.

"That we let our relationship get rundown."

"That, too."

The beginnings of a smile trembled at the corners of her lips. "That we let our l-love fall to pieces?" she offered, borrowing the phrase he'd once used to describe his new house.

No, she corrected determinedly. *Their new home.*

"I wouldn't go that far," Doug responded, quoting her words back at her.

"But still . . ." The beginnings of a smile blossomed into something very beautiful.

"You and I—our relationship needs a lot of work," Doug told her honestly. "But it's worth it, Amy. I promise you, sweetheart. It's worth it. It always has been. It always will be."

Amy lifted one of her hands and traced the lean line of his cheek and jaw. "You know," she said softly, cherishing him with her fingers. "Somebody once told me that with the right amount of time and TLC, just about anything can be salvaged."

"Really?" Doug turned his head and kissed her palm. "Did this somebody tell you anything else?"

"He . . . told me that he loved me."

"And?"

"And I believe him," Amy responded simply. "Oh, Doug—I believe him with all my heart!"

"Oh, sweetheart—"

Bending his head, Doug began brushing his lips back and forth over hers. At first the contact was so light Amy couldn't tell the difference between the caress of his mouth and the fan of his warm breath. But then he began to deepen the kiss. The feather-light brushing became a slow, sensual stroking. Amy sighed and opened to him, inviting the intimate exploration of his tongue.

Doug circled Amy with his arms and pulled her close. He made a sound deep in his throat as she moved against him. He charted the soft contours of her hips with his palms, then cupped the equally feminine curve of her bottom.

He kissed his way from her mouth to her ear, nipping and licking a tantalizing path as he went. He nuzzled through the fine strands of her copper-brown hair, then whispered, "What do you want, Amy?"

Amy gave a rippling laugh, conscious of the sweet ache in her tightening breasts and an even sweeter one between her thighs. She tilted her head back, looking into his blue eyes. "I want you, Doug," she said. "I want us to be together. I want to be your wife again." She took a deep breath, shifting her body, feeling the hard proof of his need for her. "And what do you want?"

Like her, he laughed a little at the question. Not mocking it, but rather the obviousness of part of the answer. "I want you, Amy," he told her. "I want us to be together. I want to be your husband again." He ran his hands up her back, adoring the feel of her. "We can be together wherever you choose, love. It doesn't have to be New York. It can be L.A. if you want."

Amy went up on tiptoe, stopping his flow of words by kissing the left corner of his mouth. "Now, why would I want it to be L.A.?" she inquired with a sudden spark of mischief. She could tease him a little now, now that she knew everything was going to be all right. "I never liked the city. Besides, I don't work there anymore." She smiled at Doug's start of surprise.

Doug gaped. "You what?"

Amy repeated her previous statement, then added, "I called Chaz this morning." She paused to kiss the right corner of his mouth. It was too great a temptation to resist.

"You called Chaz, and—"

"I told him I intend to quit and move back to New York to be with the man I love. The man who means more to me than any job...any deal."

"Amy," Doug began, then broke off and cupped her face in his hands. "Are you sure?"

"Oh, yes," she assured him.

She offered her mouth then, and he took it with ravishing care. The kiss was languid and long and punctuated by lazy sighs. Tongues teased and tempted. Bodies brushed and grew bold.

"Mmm..." Amy looked up at Doug when their lips finally parted. Her eyes were smoky with desire. She ran her tongue slowly over the surface of her mouth, enjoying the lingering taste of him. "Do you remember you told me you used to fantasize about my bedroom?" she asked throatily.

Doug nodded slowly.

"Well, I used to fantasize *in* my bedroom."

"Oh...really?" He gave a low laugh that sent a purr of pleasure running through her. "And what did you fantasize about?"

"Why don't you take me upstairs and find out?"

Amy undressed Doug with eager, trembling fingers. In between kisses, he did the same for her. His fingers were no less eager—and no more steady—than hers.

For a few breathless seconds, they stood, just looking at each other.

Doug drank in the sight of her, his vivid eyes dark and shimmering with emotion. "You are so...so..." He lifted his hands, palms up. There were no words to express the effect she had on him.

Amy smiled. "You are, too," she answered softly, and moved into his embrace. Going up on tiptoe, she raised her face to his.

Doug's arms came around her, holding her close. A moment later, he took what she was offering. He kissed the corners of her mouth tenderly, then traced the sweetly curving lines of it. Her lips parted and his tongue slipped between them in a gliding invasion. Amy wanted to say his name, but the only sound she made was part moan, part melting sigh.

Amy slid her hands up Doug's smoothly muscled torso, her slender fingers splayed as they tunnelled through the crisp thicket of his chest hair. She clung to him as he increased the intimacy of the kiss and stroked his tongue with her own. She felt muscles deep within her tighten and tremble in anticipation.

Doug's hands flowed up her back, then mapped out a slow, seductive path down the supple line of her spine. He charted the inward curve of her slender waist and the outward swell of her hips. Possessively, his fingers defined the cleft of her derriere, then moved lower. Amy made another inarticulate sound and shifted, feeling the heat and heaviness of his desire press against her. She wanted—needed—to be closer to him . . . and closer still.

Doug savored Amy's warmth and willingness. He wanted—needed—her so much. She was, and always would be, the only woman for him.

He murmured words of endearment and desire against her lips, trusting her to understand even if they didn't make much sense. He heard her speaking, too, and knew what she was saying even though the phrases were fragmented.

"Amy . . . Amy . . ."

"Doug . . . Doug . . ."

He kissed his way up the smooth line of her jaw, then nuzzled through the silken tangle of her coppery-brown hair to find her ear.

"Did you...did you ever fantasize about this?" he asked in a husky voice, stroking her with loving palms.

Amy shivered with pleasure, feeling the tantalizing lap of his tongue against the sensitive rim of her ear followed by the nip of his teeth on the lobe. "M-maybe...maybe once," she answered unsteadily. "Or t-twice."

Doug moved his hand one or two inches, paused, then moved it one or two inches more. A hot shaft of satisfaction lanced through him as he felt Amy shudder. "How about that?" he growled.

"Oh." Amy twisted in helpless, heart-stopping response. Her hands clenched, her nails digging into tautly muscled flesh of his shoulders. "Oh, Doug...please."

Doug bent slightly then and slipped one arm behind Amy's knees. He lifted her up and carried her over to the single bed where she had slept as a girl. He lay her down, then stretched out beside her.

To tease.

Doug ran his hands lightly over Amy's slender body, from shoulder to waist, from waist to knee, then back again. Slowly. Seductively. He finessed the tips of his fingers over the lines of her hips and stomach, then stroked upward to circle the yearning peaks of her delicate breasts. His lips curved into a fiercely tender smile as he heard Amy say his name on a quick intake of breath and saw her hazel eyes go wide with pleasure.

To touch.

Amy fitted herself against Doug, glorying in the hardened proof of his desire for her. She shifted, circling his body with her arms. She charted the stubborn jut of his jaw and the corded strength of his throat with nibbling, nipping kisses, savoring the salty tang of the perspiration on his skin as she went. She smoothed her palms down his back, her nails skimming the hard length of his spine.

To trust.

The problems of the past had been exorcised and the promises of the future lay before both of them. Yet, at this moment, the passions of the present were all that mattered.

"Oh, Amy." Doug held her. Cherished her. Offered her all he had and was.

"Oh, Doug." Amy yielded to him. Taking. Giving. Receiving. Returning. A radiant heat shimmered out from her core, making her feel as though she'd swallowed the sun.

"I need you." Doug's voice was husky, almost harsh. It was shaking a little.

"Yes. Yes," Amy affirmed, her breathing ragged.

"I want you."

"Always. Yes. Always."

"I . . . love . . . you." He kissed her between each word, unable to deprive himself of the taste and textures of her for more than a heartbeat at a time.

"I l-love you, too."

The bed was narrow. It had been comfortable for a single, slender girl. It was crowded for a grown man and woman in the throes of a passion so powerful there was no denying it.

The room swung dizzily as Doug shifted their bodies. The mattress groaned, the springs creaked. Amy clung to him. She cried out as she felt the languid, lingering search of his fingers between her thighs. He knew her intimately, utterly. Moaning deep in her throat, Amy gave herself up to the sensations he was stirring with such erotic expertise.

"Oh, oh, Doug."

And then she sought him. Found him. Clasped and caressed him.

"Amy . . . oh. Amy, sweet—"

There was no holding back. No hesitation. Amy opened completely to Doug and he took her, sheathing himself deep in her liquid heat. She surrendered; he was surrounded. Doug moved his hips. Amy shuddered and arched up against him. He moved his hips again, balancing on the razor's edge between pain and pleasure.

"Love..."

"Love..."

The room swung dizzily once again.

Reality dissolved. Time unraveled. Amy and Doug tumbled off the edge of the universe.

It wasn't until much, much later that either one of them realized they'd toppled off the bed as well.

"Doug?"

"Yes, sweetheart?" Doug dipped his head and swirled his tongue over the center of Amy's right breast.

"Did you...did you ever fantasize anything like what happened a little while ago?"

"You mean, did I ever fantasize about making passionate love to you on the uncarpeted floor of your bedroom after falling out of your extremely narrow twin bed?"

Amy gasped and clutched at him as he sucked her throbbing nipple into his mouth, then closed his teeth gently against the sensitive nubbin of flesh. After a few shivering seconds, he released the nipple and she could breathe and think and speak again.

"Y-yes," she confirmed shakily. Every fiber of her body was thrumming with the aftershocks of the ecstacy that had united them just a short time before. His continued sensual teasing made her ache for a return to that shared rapture.

"The passionate love part, absolutely," he told her with a wicked smile. "The rest—not that I remember." He turned his erotic attentions to her left breast. This time, he outlined the rosy aureole of her nipple with his tongue, making it tighten into a trembling rosette. After several moments, he raised his head to look at her. "Did you?"

"N-no." Amy shook her head. The warm lap of Doug's tongue sent quicksilver sensations arrowing through her. The sudden rake of the serrated edge of a tooth transformed those quicksilver sensations into shafts of lightning. "My fantasizes were never this—oh-oh—*Doug!*"

Doug raised his head again. His blue eyes were brilliant beneath heavy lids. "You like that?" he questioned huskily.

"I love that," Amy confessed with a voluptuous loll of her head. Then, she smiled tenderly. "But I love the man who's doing it more."

Doug smiled back, stroking his hand slowly down her body. "Hearing you say you love me is better than any fantasy," he said, feeling himself go hard with need for her once again.

"You'll be hearing it every day...and every night...from now on," Amy promised. She caressed him, gauging the smooth power of his naked body. She felt his muscles bunch in response to her touch, and savored a sense of feminine power.

"And so will you," Doug answered.

"Mmmm—" Amy closed her eyes for a few moments, letting her mind drift back. She understood it all now. Them. Him. Herself. All of it. There was nothing left to ask or wonder about except, perhaps, one dozen blush-pink roses...

"Amy?" Doug asked, feeling a sudden change in her body.

Amy opened her eyes. "You never told me," she said, nibbling her lower lip.

Doug lifted his brows. "I never told you what, Amy?"

"You never told me why you sent me a dozen blush-pink roses back in New York City."

"Ah." There was a tender secret in his smile. "That."

"You, you said something about wanting to make up for past mistakes," she recalled.

Doug nodded, gathering her close against him. Every movement he made, every breath he took, was designed to pleasure her.

"Do you remember the birthday I *didn't* send you blush-pink roses?" he asked after a moment.

Amy frowned, not really wanting to dig up an old hurt in this time of great happiness. "I remember you first gave me a bouquet of them when I turned eighteen."

"Umm-hmm," he agreed. "And I sent you bouquets of them for every birthday after that until your thirtieth. That birthday you got a dozen red roses."

"Yes," she conceded. "But—"

"Did you ever wonder why?"

Of course, she'd wondered! she thought. She'd wondered all kinds of things. Including whether he might be having an affair with another woman. Another woman who liked red roses, not blush-pink ones.

"I thought you'd probably run out of time."

"Exactly," Doug said. "I was out-of-town on business, remember? I was booked solid with appointments. Late in the day, I suddenly realized it was your birthday. I'd completely forgotten, Amy. So, in a panic, I called my secretary and asked her to send you a dozen roses. I didn't specify anything else and I told myself I didn't have time enough to do it myself."

"Oh, Doug." Amy turned her head and kissed his shoulder. She already sensed the outline of what was coming, and she was deeply touched.

Doug stroked her hair gently and shook his head, wondering how he could have been such a fool. "I can't even remember the case I was involved with at the time, Amy," he admitted. "All I recall is that I thought it was important. More important than personally taking care of my wife's birthday gift. When I began reevaluating my life after my heart attack, that episode became a symbol of what had gone wrong with us. I sent you those blush-pink roses in New York as an apology for the ones I'd once told myself I didn't have time enough to send. I also meant them as a pledge that I'll always make time enough for what's truly important in the future."

Amy lifted her face to him. "And what's going to be truly important in the future?"

He smiled. "You know."

"I know," she agreed tenderly. "But I want to hear you say it, Doug. Please."

"What's going to be truly important is you...and me. The two of us."

"And love."

"Oh, yes." He took her in his arms. "No matter what else, we'll always have time enough for love."

*   *   *   *   *

SILHOUETTE Desire™

COMING NEXT MONTH

#571 SLOW BURN—Mary Lynn Baxter
Lance O'Brien's kidnapping was over in a moment. Marnie Lee was left to deal with the aftershock—and with Lance's father, Tate O'Brien, a most enticing captor himself.

#572 LOOK BEYOND THE DREAM—Noelle Berry McCue
Erin Kennedy was surprised to land a job at a California health club—and when she met her blue-blooded boss, Logan Sinclair, she knew her wildest dreams had come true.

#573 TEMPORARY HONEYMOON—Katherine Granger
Overefficient Martha Simmons was just doing her job when she agreed to temporarily marry her boss, Jake Molloy. But once they said their "I dos," she hoped permanent love would follow.

#574 HOT ON HER TRAIL—Jean Barrett
Beth Holland was hiking the Appalachian Trail to save precious land from destruction. Opposition came in the form of sexy Brian McArdle.... Could he sidetrack Beth *and* walk away with her heart?

#575 SMILES—Cathie Linz
Classy dentist Laura Peters was haunted by fears of failure—until she met roguish Sam Mitchell, who taught her to believe in herself and to smile her doubts away.

#576 SHOWDOWN—Nancy Martin
Manhattan attorney Amelia Daniels came to Montana to find her runaway daughter and ended up in the arms of June's *Man of the Month*, charming, irascible cowboy Ross Fletcher!

AVAILABLE NOW:

A duo by Laurie Paige

There's no place like home—and Laurie Paige's delightful duo captures that heartwarming feeling in two special stories set in Arizona ranchland. Share the poignant homecomings of two lovely heroines—half sisters Lainie and Tess—as they travel on the road to romance with their rugged, handsome heroes.

A SEASON FOR HOMECOMING—Lainie and Dev's story...coming in June.

HOME FIRES BURNING BRIGHT—Tess and Carson's story...coming in July.

Come home to A SEASON FOR HOMECOMING and HOME FIRES BURNING BRIGHT...only from Silhouette Romance!